Stunt Double

OTHER BOOKS BY JEFF YAGER

Novels

Seven Days in Virtual Reality
I Like God (with Skye Bynes)
Botanica (with Fred Yager)

Young Adult (YA) Novels
Atom and Eve
A Ghostly Twist (forthcoming)

Children's Books
(Illustrated by Nancy Batra)

Chuck and Alfonzo
The Question is Why?

Stunt Double

A Novel

Jeff Yager

Hannacroix Creek Books, Inc.
Stamford, Connecticut

Published by:
HANNACROIX CREEK BOOKS, INC.
1127 High Ridge Road, #110
Stamford, CT 06905 USA
hannacroix@aol.com
www.hcbooks.us
Follow us on X (formerly Twitter):
www.x.com/hannacroixcreek

Library of Congress Control Number: 2024905135

ISBN: 978-1-938998-77-5 (trade paperback)
ISBN: 978-1-938998-78-2 (e-book)

Chapter One

A production assistant approached the trailer with the sign that read, "Cole Tillman" and knocked on the door.

"Mister Tillman?"

A few moments later, the door opened. Cole walked out and down the three steps attached to his private trailer. His was the biggest on the set. Cole was a fast-rising star on his way to the A-list. The girls wanted him, and guys wanted to be him.

"How's it going, pal?" Cole asked the assistant. "What's your name?"

"Marvin."

"Nice to meet you, Marv."

"It's time for the big fight scene," Marvin told him. "We need to shoot your scenes with Vladimir."

"Been waiting all week for this one. Let's do the damn thing!" Cole exclaimed.

They got to the set where the other actors were already in position and ready to go. They had been rehearsing for over twenty minutes. Cole took his method-acting very seriously and insisted on not rehearsing or practicing his scenes or lines with any fellow actors. He claimed that it took away from his organic reaction in the moment.

Cole walked up to his box and began to stretch. He looked over at his co-star, Vlad, who was dressed in a leather jacket, ripped jeans, and big brown boots. Cole was in a tight white tank top and beige cargo shorts.

A female production assistant approached with a clapper board.

The film director, Paul Moore, sat in a director's chair that had his name in large letters on the back. He shouted through a megaphone, "Hey Cole! Are you ready to make cinematic history?"

"My name is secret agent Troy Banks, sir," Cole responded as he pulled some dark shades out of his right cargo pocket and placed them over his eyes.

"That's what I'm talking about. A true actor," Paul Moore said. "All right, let's get this show on the road. Action!"

The production assistant held up the clapper board, saying, "Roll 5, Scene 12, Take One, Mark," and then closed it fast, making a clap noise.

Cole turned around and looked at Vlad for a moment before he said, "Where is the girl?"

"Let's just say that she is safe…for now," Vlad said as he brushed his big black beard.

"You listen here, asshole. If even one hair is harmed on her head…I will skin you alive," Cole said with vindication.

"You threatening me now?" asked the giant gangster as he slowly reached for his holster attached to his belt. "You know I got twenty guys surrounding this building ready to blast you into Swiss cheese, you know that, right?"

"And you know I'm the one guy that may be able to take on all of them, right?" Cole asked as he reached for his Uzi hidden behind his back pant line.

The two men gravitated closer and closer to one another but slowly.

"I'm just trying to get my niece back. I made a promise to my sister. So, where the hell is she?"

"If you give us what we want, you will get her back in one piece," said the tall goon.

"Is this what you're looking for?" Cole pulled a small USB drive from his left pocket.

"Is that...?" Vlad began to say as he was cut off.

"Access to all our nukes on the West Coast? Sure is."

"Hand it over, and you get your niece," said Vlad.

"Hmm, and give you access to weapons that could destroy half of Nevada? I don't think so!" Cole cocked back and launched the USB drive into an open window a few floors up.

"That was a dumb idea," said Vlad.

"Send your men now, and once they're all dead...you will bring me my niece."

"Your funeral," said Vlad as he clapped his hands. A swarm of men in black tactical gear appeared with heavy machine guns aimed at Cole.

"Cut!" the director yelled. "Get the stunt double!"

Another production assistant ran to find Johnny Biggs, who was enjoying a powdered jelly donut from the catering table. "Hey, those are supposed to be for the actors," said the production assistant.

3

"Oh, fuck off," said Johnny as he took a big bite into the jelly part of the donut. He grabbed another and put it in his cargo pants pocket.

"We need you on set. It's time for your stunts."

"Okay. Let's go," said Johnny as he made his way over to the set. He passed by a half-dozen cameras as well as big lights pointing at Cole and Vlad. Johnny walked over and gave Cole a fist bump.

"Make me look good," said Cole as he stepped aside for Johnny to take his place.

"I always do," Johnny responded, who was dressed exactly like Cole. Then he reached into his shorts pocket and grabbed his sunglasses. He put them on. They had powdered sugar from the donut on them.

"Hey, Johnny. You got something on your glass lens," one of the production directors noticed.

"Sorry about that," said Johnny as he wiped the powder off on his sleeveless shirt.

Before they could begin filming, Johnny reached into his other cargo pocket and pulled out a bottle of pills. He popped two of the white pills into his mouth. Johnny's problem with painkillers was known to the entire production crew, but no one gave him any trouble over it. Considering all of the stunts and falls he had undertaken; he was a legend on the set. He was respected despite his bad habits. Besides. Everyone knew they were prescribed by his doctor.

The other extras and stuntmen took their positions around the set that depicted a downtown district.

"All right. Let's light it up," said one of the action coordinators.

"Quiet on the set!"

Johnny stretched his knees out a bit. First the left, then the middle. He cracked his right fist's

4

knuckles before cracking the left. The painkillers were just starting to kick in.

"And action!" Paul shouted.

Johnny Biggs got into position. He looked like Cole from far away, but his distinct scar over his face was impossible to miss when close up. It must have been five inches across the bridge of his nose. Johnny had seen some things in his thirty-eight years on this planet.

The clock struck noon, and thick clouds filled the California sky.

The cameras began to roll, and the production assistant opened and shut the clapper board. Vlad stepped forward and threw a punch toward Johnny, making him dodge it, followed by two other punches, which Johnny fanned away. The other stuntmen closed in on Johnny. Vlad lifted up his prop gun and fired a couple of blanks in Johnny's direction. That's when Johnny did a quick spin kick, knocking Vlad's gun out of his hand and making it fly in the air before landing on the ground nearby. Johnny did another kick, this time into the front of Vlad's chest, knocking him back a few feet.

Cole watched from the side with some fellow actors. He took a sip of his sparkling water bottle and said, "Damn, look at me go!" He watched as Johnny performed all of his stunts.

One of the videographers panned his HD camera toward the extras and stuntmen that surrounded Johnny as he punched Vlad in his face twice, dropping him to the ground. One of the other goons ran up and tried to tackle Johnny, but Johnny dodged him making the stuntman go face first into the wall. Two other goons dressed in black tactical gear ran up, prompting Johnny Biggs to shoot his golden pistol at them, firing blanks in their direction.

The two men acted like they got shot simultaneously, both falling to the ground in agony. Another goon took off after Johnny. Johnny turned and ran toward the brick wall of the building. The man got closer just as Johnny ran up the wall and then sprung off doing a giant backflip over the other stuntman. As soon as he landed, Johnny wrapped his arm around his opponent's neck and made it look like he snapped it. The other extras started shooting at Johnny, forcing him to run in the opposite direction until he took cover behind a barricade in the street. Johnny checked the bullets in his magazine before he reloaded.

The director yelled, "Cut!"

Then they brought Cole back in to get a close-up shot of him saying a few lines. The most notable one being, *"Is that all you got?"* which was followed by a line that would be used in the movie trailer: *"You're gonna need to try harder than that!"*

After they got their closeups of Cole, the crew switched him back out for Johnny to continue the action portion of the scene. From afar, the two looked like they could be twins. Both of them were ripped from head to toe; Cole, however, got his physique with help from Hollywood's top personal trainers, while Johnny got his from a lifetime of being a legitimate tough guy. Cole Tillman had slicked-back hair that went down to his ears, so Johnny Biggs did as well.

Cole gave Johnny a fist bump before switching places with the seasoned stuntman who got behind the barricade again. Johnny waited there for a minute as the crew filmed more action sequences.

Members of the production crew were positioned on a ledge above the set. They pulled a lever, making rain fall over Johnny and the rest of the extras and stuntmen in the scene. The rain started off lightly but got heavier and heavier as the scene went on.

The sun pierced through the clouds as the director yelled, "Action!"

Johnny stood up from behind the barricade as three goons pointed their guns at him and began to fire. Johnny took off running, dodging each one of the bullets before shooting at two others.

Johnny Biggs exchanged shots back and forth with the gang of goons as they chased him around the entire movie set. Blanks were fired in each and every direction. Postproduction special effects would make it look much more spectacular in the final form.

After shooting multiple men in tactical gear, Johnny backed up into Tito, a stuntman who stood over Johnny at a whopping seven feet tall. Tito grabbed Johnny by the neck with both hands and dangled him roughly two feet off the ground.

Johnny's back and head hit the concrete when Tito choke-slammed him. Johnny lost all his breath on the fall as he committed to the scene. He wanted to make it look as painful and realistic as possible. And he succeeded as the entire cast and crew gasped in unison when Johnny hit the ground.

Tito continued choking Johnny, seemingly draining the life out of him. That's when the director yelled, "Cut! Great job, everybody!"

Tito reached his hand to lift Johnny back onto his feet.

"You all right, brother?"

"Yeah, that was great," Johnny said as he brushed the dirt off of his shoulders and gave Tito a big high five.

"You're a maniac," said Tito.

"Pleasure working with you, T, as always," said Johnny.

Other crew members from the cast came over to show their appreciation. As Johnny headed to the back locker room to get changed, Cole ran up to him to walk alongside his double.

"Man, great stuff back there, dude," said Cole.

"Thanks, Cole. Just doing my job," Johnny replied.

A production assistant called to him, saying, "Mister Biggs. We're gonna need you back on set in an hour to shoot the big gun fight scene."

"I'll be there," Johnny said.

"And Mister Tillman, we'll need you in fifteen for your monologue by the fountain."

"Got it, thanks," Cole said, turning his attention back to Johnny as they continued to walk.

"How you feeling, bro?" Johnny asked.

"Feeling great. Think this one is gonna be better than the first, by far!"

"I agree."

"Hey, listen. How about you take a trip with me to Vegas this weekend? We'll hit up all the casinos. The entire trip is on me. What do ya say?" Cole asked.

Johnny thought to himself for a moment and said, "I think I just want to get some rest this weekend, my man."

"Dude. Ya gotta fucking live a little, Biggs!"

"I appreciate the offer, Cole. But really, I'm okay," Johnny reiterated.

"How about next weekend?"

"We'll see."

"I just want to thank you for all you do," said Cole.

"You do enough for me, man. Really."

"You're too modest, Biggs. You don't have to be Humble Ol' Johnny every second, ya know?"

8

"Rain check," said Johnny. "One of these days I'll take you up on that. We'll go play some poker sometime."

"My game of choice is blackjack, but whatever Johnny wants, Johnny gets," said Cole.

"I'm well aware," said Johnny before he started to laugh.

"Great job today, John. We'll catch up soon," said Cole before he gave him a fist bump and walked away.

Chapter Two

Johnny Biggs clocked out of work at 9 o'clock that night. He left the set and headed home on his bright orange motorcycle. He lived in a suburb called Buena Park, around thirty minutes outside of Hollywood where he usually worked.

Johnny pulled up to his four-bedroom brick townhome at the end of Apple Trail. He parked his bike in the driveway and removed the key. He went to the front door and let himself in.

Once inside, Johnny put his motorcycle keys on top of the shoe case by the front door. He walked down the hallway and into the living room where his roommate, Trevor Porter, was playing his favorite video game, *League of Shooters*.

"Johnny Biggs in the house!" Trevor shouted.

"How's it going, Trev?" Johnny gave his roommate a high five.

"Living the dream, my guy. Just ranked up to level 75!"

"Wow. That's impressive," said Johnny as he walked to the kitchen. He opened the refrigerator and pulled out an ice-cold bottle of light beer.

Johnny took out his bottle of prescription pain medication. He took two pills and chased them down with some cold beer. "Ah," Johnny said to himself.

He noticed a box of pizza on the round kitchen table. Johnny opened it and saw there were three slices of pepperoni.

"You mind if I have the rest of this pizza?"

"Of course, bro, that's all you," Trevor replied from the other room.

"Hell yeah," said Johnny as he picked up a slice of pizza and took a bite.

Johnny put the other two slices on a paper plate and brought it with him to the living room. He took a seat on the other end of the couch that Trevor was sitting on. Trevor was locked into his game with his headset on, shooting at any and every opponent that came on his screen. He took his left headphone off so he could hear Johnny.

"How was filming today?" Trevor asked.

Johnny took a bite of his pizza, looked at Trevor and said, "Actually, it went really well. We shot this amazing scene. Can't wait to see how it turns out on the big screen." Johnny took another couple of bites before he got to the crust, which was his favorite part.

"Hell yeah, dawg! That's what I like to hear," Trevor replied as he bashed down the X button on his controller to shoot an enemy across the map.

"Now it's time to rest," said Johnny.

"Wanna pack a bong and watch a movie after this game?" Trevor asked.

"Sounds like a plan, my man." Johnny took another drink from his bottle of beer. "But before we do that, let me get a round in."

"All right, let me finish this game. Then you can sign in," said Trevor. "But only if you don't get us killed like last time. I'm on a winning streak!"

"I'll do my best, ya bastard," said Johnny as he took another bite of pizza.

Trevor ended the game with twenty-six kills while only dying twice. "Let's go!" he yelled as the loading screen came on. "Okay, let's get you logged in." Trevor put in the username and password for the second controller so Johnny could join him.

"Perfect, here you go," Trevor said, passing the controller to Johnny.

"Let's light these motherfuckers up," said Johnny as the next game loaded.

Johnny looked around at their vast living room. "Man, remember our last place?"

"Pshh, that one-bedroom crap hole? I slept on the couch. I remember it clearly," Trevor replied.

The two had lived in the townhouse for three years. Once the first *Bullet Town* came out, Johnny was set financially. Being Cole Tillman's reoccurring stunt double started earning Johnny between $100,000 and $200,000 a year. Johnny was raised in a lower-middle class household. His parents, Joan and Ralph, were still very close. They lived in Johnny's hometown of Reno, Nevada. Joan was a retired nurse, and Ralph had worked as a mailman at the local post office for twenty-five years before retiring with a pension.

Growing up, Johnny was kind of a shy kid, until he hit high school. That's when he found his sense of humor and learned he had the power to make his friends laugh, usually by falling or slipping on something. He figured out that he could take a fall better than most. Starting with the time in tenth grade when he tripped over a chair in the high school

12

cafeteria. The falls didn't hurt him most of the time, but everybody reacted like they did. So that stuck with him until he was much older. He knew he had a high threshold and tolerance for pain.

Johnny and his close friends in high school would film videos of themselves doing dumb stunts and pranks. He would always show off his ability for stunts. One of his favorite videos involved his friends pushing him in a shopping cart down a hill into a large tree, landing in bushes.

When Johnny graduated from high school, he followed in his dad's footsteps and became a Marine. He was stationed at Camp Lejeune in Jacksonville, North Carolina. While in the Marines, Johnny learned the martial art of Jujitsu from his good friend and fellow soldier, Ken. Johnny became quite impressive with his fighting after a couple of years of lessons on base from Ken.

After serving as a Private First Class in the military for six years, Johnny came out a changed man. He was jacked to the gills, with a ripped body that he did not have in high school. His chest and arms were much bigger. The military then paid for Johnny to attend a private stunt trade school. It was called McArthur Stunt Academy. After two years of schooling, Johnny passed his certification and obtained his film and TV stunt permit.

His first years were rough trying to find work. He even spent a couple of months living in his 2004 sedan with 200,000+ miles on it. Finally, he got some stunt work on a television show called *Scorned Earth*. That was when Johnny was able to afford the one-bedroom, where Trevor had slept on the couch. Trevor worked with Johnny at a bar and grill called *Reno's*. They both bartended together there for years.

Eventually, Johnny got assigned to do some stunt double work for Cole Tillman for a movie called *Dog Eat Dog*. Ever since, Cole had retained Johnny as his personal stunt double indefinitely. Trevor went on to become assistant manager at *Reno's*.

Lightning struck a tree nearby, making Johnny and Trevor both jump out of their couch cushions.

"Oh shit!" Trevor exclaimed. More lightning struck close to the house. Rain poured down. It had been cloudy all day, but it was the first time it had begun to rain.

Trevor and Johnny joined an exhibition online *League of Shooters* match. "Time to fry some fools," Trevor said as the game began. It was a first-person shooter. Johnny took the left side of the map, while Trevor, who specialized in sniping, found a spot northwest of the map by a stack of crates. He equipped his handgun as he looked around in a 360-degree spin. No one was in sight. Trevor switched to his sniper rifle and began scoping out enemy opponents. Johnny was much less of an advanced player. The character he was playing on the videogame walked around with an AK-47 equipped with a red dot scope.

The two played a couple of games. Trevor scored about three times more eliminations than Johnny. In between games, Trevor took a bong and packed it with some highly potent cannabis.

Trevor took a nugget of weed out of a big glass jar and said, "Bro, this shit is called Dill Pickle Haze." He then handed it over to Johnny.

Johnny took a big whiff of the sativa bud and said, "Damn! That really does smell like pickles!"

They both started to laugh hysterically.

Johnny handed the weed back to Trevor who broke it into little pieces before packing the sliding bowl. Once it was full, he placed it inside the hole, grabbed the lighter and flicked it. Trevor sucked the smoke though the tunnel of glass and held in the giant cloud of smoke for about five seconds, before coughing it all out.

After he nearly finished coughing up a lung, Trevor handed the fourteen-inch bong over to Johnny. Johnny took a swig from his bottle of beer. He held the bong in the air, then put it up to his lips and lit the bowl until smoke filled the glass. He took a smaller hit than Trevor but ended up coughing more than his roommate. The rain outside fell even harder. It sounded like bullets smacking against the roof.

Johnny moved his character through the hallways of a hotel in the game. This was Trevor's favorite level, set in Dubai. Johnny quietly approached an enemy who was turned in the other direction. He looked around in both directions before bashing the opponent in the back of the head. "Bashed that fucker!" said Johnny.

"Sick kill!" said Trevor.

Both of their eyes were halfway closed. They played a few more games as minutes turned into an hour.

Johnny took a break to grab another beer from the fridge. When he got back to the couch, Trevor had switched the input to the streaming network, Goodflix. He had selected a movie already, as the opening credits rolled down the screen.

"Oh no. Come on. Not again," said Johnny as he popped the top of the beer bottle open with a bottle opener. The cap went flying.

"Hell yeah!" said Trevor. Then, the name Cole Tillman came across the screen, followed by the movie's title, *Bullet Town*.

"Ugh. Fine," said Johnny as he sat down. He picked a slice of pizza off of his plate and took a bite.

The movie began. In the opening scene, Cole is being chased through a park. Two bad guys come up from both sides of him to attack. The camera cuts to Johnny doing a running flip to dodge both men, making them crash into each other.

"There you are!" Trevor shouted. Just as he finished speaking, the camera cut back to a closeup shot of Cole's face.

"And...I'm gone," said Johnny.

"Yeah, well I know that was really you."

In the movie, Cole gets into a striking battle with the two attackers. The camera flicks back and forth between shots of Johnny and Cole, making it hard to tell the difference between the two.

"Man, look at you go, badass mothafucka," Trevor said before laughing. "Dayum!"

"I think I'm gonna go to sleep. I'm getting pretty tired," said Johnny as he got up from the couch.

"Aww, c'mon! My bad! I can put on something else!" Trevor exclaimed.

"Nah, it's cool. Just been a long ass day. I'll catch ya in the morning," said Johnny.

He gave Trevor a fist bump and went into the kitchen. Johnny grabbed another cold beer and headed to his room. He kicked the door open, walked inside and sat on his bed. He picked up the remote control and turned on his flat screen high-definition TV. A few minutes later, Johnny fell into a deep sleep.

Chapter Three

Johnny woke up the next morning with a pounding headache. It was a quarter to nine, which meant he had a little more than an hour to get to work. He rolled out of bed. He was able to make it to the fridge in the kitchen and pulled out an ice-cold bottle of water. He unscrewed the cap and guzzled it down. He made his way back to his room where he proceeded to do a few sets of thirty pushups at a time.

After the pushups, Johnny did about a hundred jumping jacks, followed by sixty crunches, and fifty squats. He tried to stretch and work out every morning. His headache was hitting him harder by the moment. He took a drink from his water bottle.

Johnny put on some fresh jeans, along with a black belt and a plain white T-shirt. He decided to wear his old brown boots.

Then, Johnny walked out of his room and into the living room, where he found Trevor in the same spot he was in the night before. He was still playing *League of Shooters*.

"Damn, dude. Did you even get to sleep yet?" asked Johnny.

"Shoot, I think I may have gotten two or three hours of rest at most," Trevor replied. "I had a tournament this morning."

"And? How'd it go?" Johnny asked while rubbing his eyes.

"You already know your boy won that shit," Trevor replied.

"I wouldn't doubt it for a second," said Johnny.

"Wanna watch a documentary about kangaroos?"

"Ah, man. That sounds like a blast but I gotta get to work. I'm already running a little late."

"All right. Lucky me—I'm off today. Next time," said Trevor.

Johnny threw on his leather jacket, then grabbed his motorcycle keys from the shoe stand. As he walked outside to his motorcycle in the driveway, Johnny popped two painkillers into his mouth.

Johnny's first stop was the gas station. He got off of his bike, unscrewed the gas tank cap and put his debit card into the slot. He put in his PIN number and then selected the unleaded option for the fill-up.

As he was pumping his gas, a woman walked out the front door of the store. She had long blonde hair, and she seemed distracted by her cell phone. Johnny noticed a car was pulling in at the same time. It appeared as if it would hit her, but she did not notice as she was too busy texting.

Johnny shouted, "Watch out!"

The woman immediately stopped dead in her tracks as the car drove around her and into a parking spot in front of the store.

"Watch where you're going, lady!" the driver yelled out his window as he turned his car off and headed into the store.

The woman walked over to Johnny and said, "Thank you so much."

"No worries, ma'am," he replied.

The fuel nozzle stopped pumping, as the tank was finally full.

"Wait a second. I know you," said the lady. "You're Cole Tillman!"

"Oh. Uhh. Nah. I'm not..." Johnny tried to speak before she cut him off.

"I knew I recognized you from somewhere! Wow, what are the odds. Cole Tillman saved my life! I'm gonna need to get a selfie."

Johnny looked around, put the nozzle back into the holder and looked at the lady as she set up her camera on her smart phone.

"But listen, I'm not..."

"My friends are not gonna believe this. Say cheese!" she said as she started snapping selfies.

"Cheese," Johnny said begrudgingly as he smiled for the picture. The girl took a few more shots.

Then she said, "Can I see your phone?"

"Why do you want my phone?"

"Just let me see it," she said.

Johnny reached into his pocket, took out his phone and gave it to her with hesitation.

"You need to unlock it, silly" the woman said.

Johnny put his thumb on the home button of his phone, so it unlocked.

The woman then proceeded to dial her number into the dial pad. She pressed the call button. A moment later, her phone started to ring.

"There, now you have my number. Call me some time," she said as she gave him a kiss on the cheek before walking away.

Johnny looked around before he got back on his motorcycle. He put the key into the ignition and backed away from the pump. Johnny drove out of the gas station parking lot and onto the main road. He cruised for a couple of miles until he reached the entrance ramp of the highway. He was thinking about the girl he just met, trying to decide if he should call her or not.

After a thirty-minute ride, Johnny finally arrived at the studio lot.

Johnny prepared for his action scenes scheduled for that day. Then he walked over to the breakfast buffet that was reserved for the stars of the movie.

He grabbed a plate, and filled it with sausage links, bacon, and an English muffin which he buttered with a knife. Then he scooped yellow and white scrambled eggs onto his paper plate. That is when a production assistant came over. "I'm sorry, Mister Biggs, but this food is reserved for the lead actors."

Before Johnny could respond, an angry Cole, who heard the conversation from a distance, charged over. He put his arm around Johnny, looked at the production assistant and said, "Do you know who this is? How dare you try to tell this man he can't eat breakfast. He's a god damn legend, you hear?"

"Yes, sir. I'm sorry, Mister Tillman."

"Apologize," Cole demanded.

The young production assistant gazed at Johnny, then looked over to Cole. He looked back at Johnny again and said, "I'm sorry."

"Now run along. Go get me a coffee or something," Cole said.

Johnny looked at Cole and then at his plate of food. He rolled his eyes and said, "You didn't have to do that. I can handle myself."

"I know you can, bud. Just couldn't stand there and watch my main man get disrespected like that."

Johnny grabbed a plastic fork and knife, a couple of packets of ketchup, and poured a cup of orange juice from a carton on the table. He began to walk away just as Cole said, "By the way, I got something to show you after work later."

"Can't wait," Johnny said slightly sarcastically.

"You're gonna love it!" Cole exclaimed before heading back to his personal trailer.

Johnny finally got called to film some of the day's action scenes. He joined Cole who had his female counterpart and costar, Alexis Sherman, with him.

"Hey Johnny, sweetie, how are you?" asked Alexis.

"I'm doing good, Alexis. How about you? You're looking great," said Johnny.

"Oh, you're too kind. That's just what five days a week of peeling masks will do for you. As well as the countless other skin treatments they got me on," Alexis explained.

"Well, even though you don't need all that crap, you're looking great these days as always."

The film director, Paul Moore, came over to explain the next scene. "So, we have Johnny catching Alexis, whose doing her own stunt today. She'll be falling from the second story just as fire bursts through the windows."

"This is what I've been doing pushups all week for, Paul," said Johnny.

Paul laughed and said, "I wouldn't wanna fuck with you, John."

"Let's fucking do this!" Alexis exclaimed.

Johnny took a sip from his water bottle and nodded in agreement.

The lead stunt coordinator got all the cast for the scene ready and in position. A couple of fire effects specialists were in the building setting Alexis up in a safety harness that was connected to a strong steel wire.

"Cameras rolling. Let's get ready to shoot in 5...4...3...2... action!" shouted the head of videography.

An explosion rang out from inside the building, shattering window glass. At the same time, Alexis dove out of the burning building through one of the windows, twenty feet in the air, flying directly into Johnny's arms. Johnny caught her but not without completely tumbling backwards. He almost did a full backflip onto his head but thankfully he protected her on his way down.

Johnny got back onto his feet, still holding Alexis in his arms. One of the main cameras panned around the two as they stood there for a moment. Johnny held her in the air, and it felt like time had frozen.

"Cut!" Paul shouted. "That was fantastic. But now we have to replace Johnny with Cole for the big kiss shot."

"Aww, man. Would have preferred to kiss Johnny," the beautiful Alexis said before winking at him.

Johnny smiled as he continued to hold her until Cole could get there.

Cole walked up to them and said, "Fine by me, not like I really wanna kiss you anyway."

Alexis laughed and said, "Lighten up."

Johnny handed her to Cole and walked off behind the camera setup.

"That was awesome, Johnny," Cole said as he struggled to hold Alexis up with ease the way that Johnny did.

"I appreciate that, Cole," Johnny replied.

"Everybody ready? Quiet on the set. And action!" the director yelled.

Cole leaned Alexis back a bit and said, *"You know I got you, baby!"*

The two kissed dramatically and romantically as the wind fans blew leaves in the air behind them. Johnny watched with a face of slight disgust. Cole kissed Alexis for nearly twenty seconds before Paul Moore yelled, "End scene!"

"How was that?" Cole asked the director.

"Fan-fucking-tastic!" Paul replied. "Let's just run it back two more times. That was excellent."

After a long day of shooting, it was closing time for the cast and crew as they wrapped up for the day. Johnny took a hot shower in the male locker room. Once he was finished, he dried and grabbed his duffel bag from his locker. Johnny made his way to the parking lot.

As he got closer to his motorcycle, he noticed that Cole was standing by what appeared to be a brand new bright blue SUV.

Johnny walked over and said, "Damn. Nice wheels you got there."

"It is nice, right? It's a hybrid Pompa 4-wheel drive!" Cole said with excitement in his voice.

"That's really sick, bro. I'm happy for you," said Johnny.

"Well, actually you should be happy for yourself. Because it's yours. This is the surprise I was telling you about. I wanted to show you my appreciation for all you do for me. Well, really for us!"

"You didn't have to do that, Cole." Johnny walked around and looked at the car in amazement.

"I know I didn't, but I just wanted to do something nice for you. You make me look like a badass and that makes you the baddest of asses," said Cole before he threw the keys in the air and Johnny caught them.

He gave Cole a hug, smiled big, and said, "Not sure what I'm gonna do with my bike, though."

"You ride the bike home; I'll have one of the production assistants drop off the car. You earned it, my friend. Keep up the great work and there's much more where that came from."

"You're the man," Johnny said as he got on his motorcycle. A production assistant walked over, and Johnny handed him the keys to his brand-new hybrid SUV. Still feeling amazed, Johnny rode his motorcycle out of the studio lot parking lot.

Chapter Four

A week later, Johnny sat at the end of the couch watching Trevor play live esports tournaments of *League of Shooters*. Johnny was off work for the weekend. It was almost noon.

Trevor got second place in a silver rank free-for-all. "Dammit! I should've had that one."

"You'll get the next one, I'm sure," Johnny replied. He pulled out his phone, pressed his thumb against the home screen and opened it up. Johnny clicked on the Holler button. Holler was a new hip dating app that Cole recommended he download. Johnny hoped to find someone who wanted to go out with him, not like the blonde from the gas station who was only interested because she thought he was Cole.

He swiped right on a woman with brown hair down to her shoulders.

He swiped left on a girl he didn't find too attractive, but then he swiped right on the next one. Swiping right meant that you wanted to match with them and swiping left meant you were denying them. Johnny used the app for about twenty minutes. He was looking for a possible date with a woman he might have a spark with. It had been nearly a year since his breakup with Lisa, his former girlfriend.

Johnny and Lisa had dated for a little more than two years. Lisa did not really approve of Johnny's line of work. It scared her every day he went to the set like he was a police officer or firefighter going into the line of duty. She hated to see him get hurt or put himself in various dangerous situations.

Johnny and Lisa grew very close, but Lisa was six years younger than Johnny. She was not ready to have children, while Johnny thought that he was. After a while, Johnny decided to break up. He figured that he was doing her a favor. He told himself that if it was meant to be then they would find each other down the road. He still loved Lisa but could not continue the way things were going when they both had very different goals. Johnny would reach out to Lisa from time to time to see how she was doing. He stopped checking in so frequently when he saw on social media that she was in a new relationship with a lawyer.

"Oh snap!" Johnny exclaimed.

"What happened?" Trevor asked.

"Just matched with one of the most beautiful girls I've ever seen," Johnny said.

"No way. Let me see," said Trevor as he took his eyes off the game for the first time in a while.

Johnny handed him his phone. "Dayum! You ain't lying! Jane, huh? She's fine as hell."

"Right?" Johnny said.

"To be honest, she probably thinks she just matched with Cole Tillman," Trevor said before bursting out laughing. Just then, he got bashed in the head in the game and got killed. "Shit!" he yelled. He rarely got killed in *League of Shooters*.

"Ha! That's what you call instant karma," Johnny said.

Trevor passed the phone back to him. "I'm just playing. But you better make sure that ain't no catfish. That girl is super-hot. Might be a creepy dude or some shit."

"I sure as hell hope not. Should I send her a message?"

"Nah. Matching is good enough. Might as well call it a day. —Are you serious? Of course, send her a message, my guy!" Trevor exclaimed as he began bashing the buttons on his controller. He was having an epic shootout with one of the enemy players. He ended up winning the battle by shooting him with a shotgun in the face.

Johnny sat back on the couch and tried to get comfortable. He clicked the *send message* button and typed: "What's going on? My name is Johnny." He followed it up with a winky face emoji.

A few minutes passed as he waited with anticipation. Then Johnny got an alert notification on his lock screen. Jane had responded to his message on the Holler app.

Johnny got a little bit nervous and told Trevor, "Yo, she just replied."

"Well, what did shorty say?" Trevor asked.

"Hold up. Let me see." Johnny opened the app and read her response.

"Hey there, Johnny. How are you doing this beautiful afternoon?" Jane wrote. She added a blushing face emoji.

Johnny read the message out loud for Trevor.

"Bro! She wants you! She sent you that emoji? You got this in the bag, my G," Trevor said in excitement.

Johnny went on to message Jane back and forth for quite a bit of time until Johnny smoothly told her, "I don't like being on this app longer than I need to.

27

How about you text me?" He then sent her his number.

A few minutes later, he got a text from a new number that read, "Hey cutie, it's Jane."

The two texted back and forth throughout the day until Johnny finally built up enough courage to ask her out on a date. Jane agreed that they should meet up.

They made plans to go out the following day. Johnny suggested a great restaurant in the area, Massimo's. It was an elegant and decadent spot he always wanted to take Lisa to, but they never got the chance to go before things ended. Jane lived only twenty minutes away, so Johnny offered to pick her up.

"It's a date!" Jane texted Johnny.

"Can't wait," Johnny replied.

The next day, Sunday, Johnny stayed busy by working out and doing some chores around the house. Trevor helped with bills, but he was not the cleanest roommate. Johnny was a bit more OCD about getting things done around the house. He spent several minutes scrubbing and cleaning gunk off of the plates, bowls, and silverware that had piled up in the sink.

Later that day, Johnny took his brand new Pompa SUV to the grocery store. He needed a few items for the house, such as milk, eggs, chicken, pork, steak, a bag of white rice, a case of water, paper towels, and some fruits, and veggies. He got back to his new car in the parking lot. He pushed the trunk button on the key so that it was already open by the time he got there.

The sky was as blue as the ocean waves, with pure white clouds floating by calmly. He drove the car over to the gas station so he could fill up the tank. The last stop he made was the outbound mailbox outside of the post office so he could send his parents an envelope containing signed pictures of all the stars of *Bullet Town*. They were not just proud of Johnny and all of his career accomplishments, but they were actually really big fans of the movie, especially his father. Johnny put the envelope inside the mailbox before driving off in his Pompa. He was all done with his errands. He figured he would get back home and freshen up for his date that night.

After a hot shower, proper teeth brushing and a quick beard trim, it was time for Johnny to pick out his outfit for the night. He opened his closet and looked through his shirts on the hangers. Nothing stuck out to him, and he was having trouble deciding what to wear. Finally, he chose a multicolored button-down shirt that had shades of green and grey throughout. "That's the one," he said to himself. He chose a white tee shirt to wear as an undershirt. Then he grabbed his preferred dark blue jeans and the nicest black shoes he had. Johnny grabbed his favorite cologne, *Redemption*, and sprayed his wrists before rubbing them together. Then he sprayed his chest and stomach area before adding a spritz to both sides of his neck. He rubbed it in before it could drip onto his nice shirt.

At 7:30 P.M., Johnny pulled up to the address that Jane had sent him. It was a cute duplex down Sycamore Lane about twenty minutes from Johnny's house.

"Hey, I think I'm here," Johnny texted Jane. A minute later, he got a response. "Be right out."

Johnny checked himself in the mirror as he nervously waited to meet her for the first time.

He pulled out his prescription bottle. Johnny shook it up a bit before popping off the cap and ingesting three pain pills. "C'mon, Johnny. You got this. Don't be an idiot, you're the fucking man," he said to his reflection in the rear-view mirror.

He turned up the volume on the radio as one of his favorite alternative rock songs played. It was called "Yoga" by The Satellites. The melody helped calm his nerves.

Minutes went by. Johnny got more and more nervous as sweat dampened his cheek and his palms grew clammy.

That's when the front door of the duplex opened. Jane walked out and down the steps and over to the car. She was even more beautiful to him in person than in her pictures, which was hard for him to even believe. She had dirty blonde hair, and wore square glasses, a bright red dress, black and red high heels, and had a fancy brown purse on her shoulder. She looked like she had makeup on, but not too much.

Johnny paused for a moment, frozen in place by her beauty, before he realized he should get out of the car and introduce himself.

He opened the driver-side door and scurried over to give Jane a friendly hug. He wasn't really sure what to do. It had been a while since he had gone on an actual date. "You look...amazing," he said nervously.

"Thank you, honey," Jane responded. She kissed him on the cheek. There was an awkward moment of silence before she added, "So are you gonna let me in or what?"

"Of course, what am I thinking?" Johnny opened the passenger side door and helped her into her seat.

"What a gentleman," she said before smiling.

Johnny shut the door and went to the other side of the car. He hopped into the driver's seat. He locked the doors and buckled his seatbelt. She then buckled hers as well.

"Nice car! Impressive," said Jane as she looked around at the interior. "It even has that new car smell. Did you just get it?"

"Actually, yes I did," Johnny said. He did not want to bring up the fact that Cole bought it for him. At least not right away. He was enjoying how she seemed really impressed as she looked around at the car's features and details.

"This must have cost a fortune," she said as she felt the soft texture of the car walls.

"Definitely a pretty penny," Johnny replied as he put the SUV in reverse and pulled out onto the road.

The two were seated in a terrific spot at Massimo's at a round table directly in the middle of the packed restaurant.

Johnny ordered a bottle of Merlot for the table. The waiter brought them both glasses of water. Jane ordered the chicken marsala, while Johnny ordered their famous lasagna.

The two got to know each other as the night went on and they waited for their food. Chemistry was building. They were hitting it off.

The waiter brought over their dishes.

"Oh, yum!" Jane said as she looked at her plate. She pulled out her smart phone and took a couple of pictures.

"Don't judge me," she said as she snapped photos of the food.

"Never," Johnny responded. He took his fork and cut a piece of his lasagna. He took a bite, and immediately he felt like his taste buds were dancing.

"How is it?" Jane asked as she cut a piece of her chicken.

"Best. Lasagna. Ever," he replied.

"Oh my gosh, you're gonna have to try this chicken marsala! So good!" she exclaimed.

They ate and ate until they were both almost too full to walk.

"I have a confession to make," said Jane.

"Oh no, here we go. I knew it was too good to be true," Johnny said before laughing.

"No. Well. I just have to be honest. When we first matched, I could have sworn that you were that actor, you know, Cole Tillman," she said.

"Ah, right. That makes sense," Johnny said as he wiped sauce from his face with a napkin.

"And when I found out you weren't him, I almost just straight up ghosted you. I thought maybe you were using a fake name or something since it was on Holler. But once I got to know you more, I just want to say. I really like you, Johnny. For you," Jane explained.

Those words were music to his ears.

"What do you say we finish off the night at your place?" Jane asked.

"I think that's an outstanding idea," Johnny said. "Waiter! Check please!"

Jane looked at him from across the table with eyes that could make him melt.

After dinner was over, the two headed back to Johnny's house where Jane ended up staying the night. As the night progressed, they got closer, emotionally, romantically, and physically.

Chapter Five

Johnny was on the movie set in a forest of trees, being chased by his fellow stuntmen dressed in pitch black tactical suits. He was running at full speed, weaving in and out of the pines. Johnny looked back and saw that one of the goons was gaining on him. He leaped over a downed tree before jumping off of another that lay ahead.

Multiple cameramen followed Johnny as he performed his live action tour through the forest.

A helicopter came out of nowhere, flying above Johnny as it chased him through the woods.

The lead stunt coordinator for the scene, Owen, followed closely along making sure that each action sequence went the way it was supposed to. He seemed pleased with the art that they were creating. One of the videographers got in for a closer shot. That's when Eddy, another stuntman, ran up to Johnny with a gun pointed directly at him. Johnny noticed this in his peripherals and countered the attack with a moment's notice. Just when Eddy got close enough, Johnny used one foot to catapult himself off of a wide pine tree, and then spin-kicked Eddy across the face with the other.

This made Eddy do a 360-degree flip in the air before crashing down to the ground.

The whole production team gasped in unison at the stunt. Johnny and Eddy nailed it perfectly. You could see the excitement on Owen's face.

Johnny continued to run. Cole was watching from the side, preparing for the moment the director would call him in for his shots. Bullets sprayed from the helicopters forcing Johnny to duck behind various trees that surrounded him. That's when one of the trees snapped apart at the bottom near the root. Johnny was running right toward it as it toppled. At the last second, Johnny dodged the giant lumber before it crushed him to pieces.

The entire crew watched in anticipation, praying that Johnny would not be hurt during the action, especially Cole. Once they knew Johnny was all right, the crew was able to breathe a sigh of relief.

Another stuntman in black tactical gear propelled down a wire from the helicopter. Johnny noticed this and shimmied up a tree to meet the attacker halfway. As the attacker got lower on the wire, Johnny jumped off the left branch of the tree and hooked onto the wire the man was hanging from. He pulled himself up like it was a rope, until he was face-to-face with the incoming attacker. The suited man shot at Johnny, but Johnny was able to dodge the shots before knocking the man's gun from his hands, sending it flying through the air.

Johnny grabbed the man and pulled him from the wire, making him fall nearly twenty feet to the ground. Johnny then jumped off, soaring to the ground, landing on the man. He gave one hard punch to the man's face before running away from the helicopter again.

The director yelled, "Cut!"

Paul Moore hurried to Johnny to give him a high five.

"That was some great shit!" said Paul.

"Cole, we need you for closeups."

Cole gave Johnny a fist bump before they switched places.

Johnny walked off behind the camera and production crew. A production assistant handed him an ice-cold water bottle.

"Thanks," Johnny said as he took the bottle, popped the cap off, and guzzled it down.

After he chugged almost the entire bottle of water, Johnny reached into his pocket and pulled out his bottle of prescription painkillers. He swallowed three pills all at once. His back had been hurting. Might have been due to a bad fall he took on set recently when one of the other stuntmen slammed him wrong. He had not been sleeping well ever since. He justified to himself that the pain pills helped him tolerate his injuries from the different stunts and action sequences.

Later that afternoon, filming wrapped for the day. Trevor pulled up to the studio parking lot in Johnny's new SUV. He found Johnny waiting by the curb with his duffel bag.

The blue Pompa shined bright in the parking lot. Trevor unlocked the car doors just before Johnny hopped in the front passenger seat.

"What up, Biggsy?" asked Trevor.

Johnny strapped in his seat belt and said, "Just living the dream, bro. How was your day?"

"Pretty good, dawg. It's my day off so you know for a fact I was capping fools in *League* all morning," Trevor said.

He put the car in reverse and pulled out of the studio parking lot.

The late afternoon sun shone bright over Los Angeles as Trevor and Johnny cruised down the busy street toward their city. A black and yellow taxicab merged from Main Street out of nowhere, nearly crashing into the side of the Pompa. Trevor was able to swerve at the last second.

"Watch where you're going, asshat!" Trevor yelled out of the window.

The taxi drove off.

"Good job avoiding that dickhead," said Johnny.

"I ain't gonna let anything happen to this beauty," Trevor said.

"I can tell," said Johnny.

"You getting hungry?"

"Actually," Johnny began to say as his stomach rumbled. "I can definitely eat something. Pretty hungry."

"Okay, word. I heard about this new little hipster spot about ten minutes from the crib. Apparently, they have the best pasta ever. And good soups, too," Trevor went on.

"Sounds great. Let's do it."

Trevor turned up the volume as the song "Catch a Body" came on the radio. It was by a rapper named Litty Smitty.

"Fuck yeah! This is my jam!" Trevor shouted as the bass tumbled through the large car. Johnny was unfamiliar with the song, but he began to nod his head up and down to the beat.

"Not too bad," Johnny said as the song grew on him the longer it played.

After driving for about twenty minutes in and out of traffic, Trevor and Johnny pulled up to the restaurant. It was a little hole-in-the-wall spot called "The Roost" and it was gaining more and more popularity recently.

"How the hell did you even hear about this place?" asked Johnny.

"My boy Dan told me about it. I guess he took his girl there last week. He told me I gotta try it. And Dan knows food."

Trevor found a parking spot on the street nearby. There were multiple tables out in front of the restaurant. It was quite busy for such a small location.

The weather was beautiful, so Trevor asked for a table for two on the outside patio. They lucked out as a small table had just opened up due to a cancellation.

"Right this way," said the host as he led them to their table.

Johnny and Trevor took a seat at their cloth-covered table. Their waitress brought them two cups of ice water.

"My name is Eliza, and I will be your waitress today. I'll be right back with some menus and to tell you about our daily specials," she said.

"Sounds great," said Johnny.

The waitress blushed and winked at Johnny before walking away.

"Did you see that?" Trevor asked.

"What's that?" Johnny asked before taking a sip of his water.

"Dude, she totally wants you. She just winked at you and everything," said Trevor.

"Pfft, she probably just thinks I'm Cole. It's happening more and more lately."

"And? So? If I looked like a famous actor, I'd be pulling girls left and right," said Trevor.

"Yeah, well, that's not how I want to do it."

"I get it, man. But still. Use that shit to your advantage!"

"I'd rather a girl want me for *me*, you know what I'm saying?" Johnny replied. "I may have already met her. Jane is actually pretty cool. I don't know, we'll see."

"I get it. I get it," said Trevor.

Eliza brought over two menus and asked, "Is there anything besides water you would like to drink?"

"I'll take a cola," said Johnny.

"Same," Trevor added.

"Also, just to fill you guys in on our specials, we have tomato bisque for our soup of the day. And our entree of the day will be the jambalaya. It's got a bit of a kick to it, but it is absolutely tremendous," Eliza explained.

"Dang, that does sound pretty banging," said Trevor.

"Also, new on the menu is our chicken, bacon, and avocado club. That's also really good," the waitress said. "But I'll let you guys go over the menu for a bit and I'll be right back out with your sodas."

"We appreciate it," said Johnny.

Johnny and Trevor both glanced at their individual menus. They had quite a bit to choose from.

"Man, everything looks great. I don't know what to pick," said Johnny.

"I know, right? Same," Trevor replied.

They both took a little bit of time to examine the menu.

Sitting next to them was a table of four. It appeared to be a mother with her three children. Two boys and a girl. They were a bit loud, having fun chatting and eating. Johnny could hear the two older brothers pick on their sister. The kids all appeared to be under the age of ten. The mother looked to be enjoying a mimosa. Johnny found her fairly attractive. She had long brunette hair with blonde highlights. He wondered if the father was in the picture. Then he snapped back to reality and continued to read the menu. He still had no idea what to order.

The waitress returned a couple of minutes later with a tray holding two glasses of cola with ice.

"Why thank you, Eliza," said Trevor.

"My pleasure," she responded. "So, what did we decide on?"

Trevor put the menu down on the table and exclaimed, "I think I'm gonna go with the jambalaya!"

"Great choice," the waitress said as she wrote into her little pad. "And how about you?" she asked as she turned to Johnny and smiled.

"Well... I think I'm gonna get the cheeseburger and fries. Can I get that with Gouda? And extra pickles, please?"

"Of course, honey," she said. "I'll have all of that right out to you boys."

Eliza walked away. Trevor turned to Johnny and asked, "So, how was shooting today?"

"Pretty good. We shot this pretty sick scene. I'm excited to see how it turns out," Johnny responded.

"Hell yeah!" Trevor exclaimed. "I bet it's gonna be the shit."

"Ha, we'll see how it comes off on screen," Johnny said. He took a gulp from his glass of cola.

Just then, a big gray van pulled up in front of the restaurant. At first, Johnny and Trevor did not notice it. Then, the back of the van opened up wide. Moments later, two men in black ski masks and white hooded sweatshirts hopped out of the back and headed toward the front patio of The Roost. That is when Trevor took note of the strange men. One of them was

40

way taller than the other one, more than six feet tall. Johnny looked up.

The two masked men targeted the table next to them with the mom and three kids. Trevor's jaw dropped as the shorter man ran over and brazenly grabbed the little girl. The taller one helped him as they dragged her from her chair and away from the table.

The mom shrieked. "Help! They're taking my daughter!"

At first, Johnny was frozen in shock. He was unable to move. It was as if it was all happening in slow motion. Fellow patrons of the restaurant did not know what to do, but some of them pulled out their phones to record the incident. The mother cried for help one more time, "Please! Somebody help! Call the police!"

That's when Johnny realized he had to do something. He leaped over the railing that separated the patio from the sidewalk. The men continued to drag the girl to the back of the grey van.

Johnny raced as fast as he could until he got a few feet away from the van. The two masked men turned around only to be met with the bottom of Johnny's feet. One for each of their faces as Johnny drop kicked them both into the van. This caused them to release the girl who fell to the ground.

Johnny then picked her up and ran the little girl back to her mother and brothers. Onlookers continued to catch the whole scene on their smart phones. There must have been at least four people recording the situation going down.

He made sure the little girl was safe with her mom before he turned around and ran back toward the kidnappers. But by that time, their van had sped off and away from the restaurant. Johnny made a note of the license plate: *UDA-574*. He also noticed a weird logo/emblem, it was hexagon shaped. He had never seen it before, but it caught his eye.

Johnny pulled out his phone and typed the plate number in his notepad app.

After all was said and done and the van had disappeared, Johnny made his way back to his table. When he sat in his chair, every customer began cheering for him. Some of them were still filming. He looked around and noticed everyone was clapping. Trevor stood up and yelled, "That's my man!" He then high-fived Johnny.

Eliza said, "Wow! That was incredible!" She smiled at Johnny.

Then, the mother of the children walked over holding her daughter's hand. She looked at Johnny and said, "Thank you, sir. You saved her life. How can I ever repay you?"

"Oh, it's okay," Johnny said humbly. "I'm just glad I could help."

"If there is anything I can ever do for you, just let me know," said the mother as she reached into her purse and pulled out a business card.

Johnny took her card and read her name, "Melissa Carlson."

"I'm a masseuse," said Melissa.

"Well actually, I may need you at some point. My back has been killing me," said Johnny.

"Any time. It's on the house," she said. Then, the little girl looked up at Johnny and said, "Thank you for saving me, Mister."

She then hugged Johnny. But the gravity of the situation hadn't even settled in yet. Johnny was still in a state of shock from the whole ordeal.

The waitress brought over a tray full of food. She handed Johnny his plate with the cheeseburger and said, "Here you go, hero." She smiled and then gave Trevor his bowl of jambalaya.

"Thank you," said Johnny. His stomach growled as he picked up the burger and looked at it for a second before taking a big bite into the middle of the bun. "Damn, that's good," said Johnny as he let the taste rest on his pallet.

Trevor smelled his bowl of rice, spices, chicken, shrimp, and andouille sausage. The aroma passed from the table into the air and around them. Trevor then stuck his fork into the jambalaya and took a big bite. "Delicious!" he exclaimed.

"You were right. This place is great," said Johnny.

People continued to watch Johnny from their tables in amazement at what they had just witnessed on the street in front of The Roost.

"Ya know, what you just did was incredible," said Trevor as he continued to eat.

"It was nothing," Johnny replied. He took another bite into the burger.

"Nah, bro. You were a real-life superhero. That was the craziest shit I ever seen," said Trevor.

"Just doing what I felt was necessary," said Johnny.

"That was wild. You're the man," Trevor said with certainty. "Proud to call you my best friend."

Distant police sirens grew louder.

"Better eat quick, my man," Trevor told him. "Those cops will be wanting to talk to you."

Chapter Six

Later that night, Johnny tossed and turned in his bed, trying to sleep. He would doze for ten minutes at a time and then wake back up. He kept having flashbacks to earlier in the day when the attempted kidnapping occurred.

Around 2 A.M, Johnny grabbed his bottle of pills off of his nightstand. He unscrewed the cap and popped one pill into his mouth and washed it down with a sip from the water bottle that he always kept next to his bed at night.

Finally, Johnny was able to find some slumber just before 3 A.M. Unfortunately, he was woken up twenty minutes later when Trevor yelled from the other room, "Yo! John! You awake?"

Johnny was startled and immediately sat up.

"I am now!" He rubbed his eyes. "What's up, Trev?"

"You gotta come here, bro!"

Johnny rolled out of bed in his tank top and boxer shorts. His eyes were still blurry as he stumbled into the hallway.

He walked down the dark hallway toward the screen-lit living room. He could hear the sounds of shots firing from down the hall. This was nothing new to Johnny. He entered the living room and found Trevor with his eyes wide open staring at the large, big screen flat screen TV mounted to the wall.

"Damn, bro. You gonna go to sleep at any point?" Johnny asked.

"One day," Trevor replied before laughing.

"What's going on, man? I just fell back asleep. I hope this is good," Johnny said.

"My man, have you not been on the internet tonight? Nobody reach out to you yet?"

"What do you mean?" Johnny asked. He then walked into the kitchen, cracked open the refrigerator, and pulled out an ice cold can of cola.

From the other room, Johnny could hear Trevor yell out, "Oh my god! Dude!"

Johnny took a sip of his cola after it finished fizzing. He walked back into the living room.

"What is it?" Johnny asked. He settled on the sofa.

"You've gone viral, homie!" Trevor exclaimed. In his game, he snuck up behind an enemy and performed a melee attack with his rifle.

"What do you mean?"

"I mean on the internet. Your video is everywhere!"

"No way, really?"

"For real! I saw it posted in multiple angles and video uploads on StreamTube. And it's already all over social media. Two of my friends posted it on MyFace. I couldn't believe my eyes. I was like, that's my fuckin boy!"

"I don't believe you," Johnny said, still very tired and only slowly coming to the realization of what his roommate/best friend was telling him.

"Dude, come here and look," said Trevor. He pulled out his smartphone and opened the StreamTube app. After it loaded, Trevor clicked on the video and handed the phone to Johnny.

Johnny watched himself jump up from the restaurant table and run over to drop-kick the kidnappers before bringing the girl back to her mother. The scene unfolded from one of the onlookers' angles.

"Holy shit," Johnny said aloud. The video ended with the small crowd of people erupting into applause. So far, the video had garnered 540,000+ views in less than a day's time.

"Crazy, right?" Trevor said as he went back to playing his game. "And that's only one angle that was uploaded. I've seen two others already!"

"Can't believe it," said Johnny. "Thanks for letting me know."

"I thought you'd like that," Trevor said excitedly. "You're gonna be all over the net by tomorrow, just watch."

"I guess we'll see," said Johnny.

He got up off the couch, gave Trevor a fist bump and said, "I'm gonna go back to sleep, homie. See you in the morning."

"Goodnight, hero," Trevor said before shooting one of the enemies in the game.

"Goodnight my G," Johnny responded. He left the living room and headed back down the hallway. He opened the door to his bedroom and walked inside. He fell down on his bed and curled up into his blanket. He wanted to check his MyFace account to see if anyone sent him anything or tagged him in the video, but he was too tired and decided to look in the morning. Within minutes, Johnny fell back asleep.

The next morning, Johnny woke up around 8:35 A.M. Once he came to full consciousness, Johnny rolled over in his bed and grabbed his phone which was lit up on his nightstand.

He looked at the home screen and saw that he had over twenty missed calls and fifteen text messages from various friends, coworkers, and family.

"What in the world?" Johnny said to himself. He also noticed that he had multiple notifications that he was tagged in posts and comments on MyFace.

Johnny opened up the MyFace app on his phone and clicked the notifications button. His eyes lit up from the screen. He saw that his childhood friend, Marcus, had tagged him in a comment on the video someone had uploaded to the social network. He also saw that his cousin, Judy, made a post sharing the video where she tagged him as well. He looked in his inbox on the app and saw that many friends online had messaged him telling him they saw it. He listened to a few voicemails from friends and family, including his parents. Everyone was supportive and proud in their messages and comments. Johnny then saw that one of the uploaded videos of the incident had just under a million views already (895,533 to be exact) which were growing by the minute. More and more people seemed to be sharing the video or reposting it themselves. There were four different angles from four different phones uploaded.

"Damn, Trev was right," he said to himself. "I guess this is what it means to go viral."

Johnny started reading the comments, barely containing his excitement.

He came across one comment from an anonymous user online that read, "Holy Crap! That's amazing! Is that Cole Tillman?!"

Another user responded to the user's comment by writing, "I thought so too! But after a bit of research, it appears to be his stunt double, Johnny Biggs!"

Another reply to the comment read, "Great Job Johnny!"

One of the comments read, "From stuntman to real life action hero!!"

Johnny began to blush as he did not realize what an impact his action would have, let alone that the whole world would be able to see it. He did not really know how to feel. But the comments were flattering him.

He got out of bed and left his room. He entered the bathroom and sat on the toilet. He continued to read comments, posts, and messages. He couldn't stop smiling. Once he finished his business on the toilet, he shaved and brushed his teeth. When he left the bathroom, he went back to his room. He got motivated to do some pushups. Then he switched to sit-ups.

After getting ready for the day, Johnny realized he did not have much planned. It was his day off from shooting. He figured he would get a few chores and errands done.

Johnny took the Pompa to the grocery store to get some things for the house. He knew he needed a case of water, a gallon of milk, and a carton of eggs.

Johnny pulled into the Shop & Go parking lot and found a spot fairly close to the entrance.

Once inside, Johnny grabbed a shopping cart and pushed it around the store, investigating the different aisles. He found himself by the juice section, trying to decide on a juice for the house. He ended up grabbing a carton of orange juice, as well as a carton of pineapple berry punch. That was his favorite.

He loaded up the cart with spinach, green peppers, onions, a head of lettuce, carrots, zucchini, squash, and some kale. Then he made his way toward the butcher side. He threw a package of boneless chicken thighs into the cart. Then he found some NY strip steaks as well.

While he was selecting some pork chops, he noticed there were two men who looked like they could be part of a mafia family. They were both dressed in white button-down shirts with ties and they both had goatees. Johnny got a weird vibe from them. He thought they were following him up and down the aisles. But after a while, he snapped out of it and concluded that he was just being paranoid. He continued on with his shopping and ignored the men. Finally, he turned around and they were nowhere in sight.

Johnny walked down aisle 12, where the cereal was located. He grabbed a box of Frosted Flats, which was his favorite brand. Johnny's stomach began to growl, his hunger growing strong. It was most likely due to being surrounded by so much food in the store. He selected a rotisserie chicken by the hot food section. Lastly, before leaving, he stopped for his prescription refill at the pharmacy. Johnny then headed to the checkout line.

Johnny left the store with a cart full of shopping bags of food. He was quite angry at the cost of everything coming out to over $210 when he felt like he barely got enough food to last him a whole week.

He got back to the SUV and popped the trunk with the button on his keys.

Johnny filled up the trunk with bags of groceries and shut the door. Then he hopped into the driver seat and drove to his next errand.

He made a left onto Grapevine Road and continued straight for a while. He turned up the volume on the radio as it was playing one of his favorite songs, "Orange Sunset" by The Rackets when his phone started to ring. He looked at the front screen and saw that it was Cole. He turned the volume knob down on the radio.

"What's going on, Cole?"

"Dude! I saw the video!" Cole shouted through the phone's speaker.

"And? What are your thoughts?" Johnny replied.

"Oh man. That was fucking amazing. You were incredible, bro! I never seen any shit like that before," said Cole.

"I appreciate that, thank you," Johnny responded.

"I'm seeing that video posted everywhere, man. At first, people thought it was me!" Cole said before laughing.

Johnny laughed, too. "It wouldn't be the first time, ha-ha."

"Bro, for real. That was some real G shit. I couldn't believe my eyes. You really saved that girl's life. That was crazy!" Cole exclaimed.

"Just did what I could. Sucks that they got away. Wish we caught them," said Johnny.

"Yeah, man. Just a word of advice. Stay true to yourself. No matter what they say or do going forward," said Cole.

"Right. Not sure what you mean, really."

"Well, just saying. Be prepared. People may treat you a bit differently now that you're going to be a viral sensation and shit. Who knows what's to come, you know what I mean?" Cole asked.

"Yeah, I think so," Johnny said in a confused tone.

"Well. Just remember, you're my boy for life. And I always got your back. Every movie I got coming up, I'm gonna need you. You know that," said Cole.

"Of course, my man. I got you."

"All right, well I gotta run. Ima hit you up soon. Again, that was amazing. You're a hero bro. For real," said Cole.

"Thanks, Cole. That means a lot. So are you, my man. You're the real hero," Johnny replied.

"Nah. That's you," Cole said.

"Well only with your help, my man," Johnny said. "Talk to you soon."

"All right, dawg. Talk to you later."

They both hung up at the same time.

Johnny came to a red light and turned the volume back up on the radio.

Chapter Seven

Johnny bench pressed a bar with two large circular weights on each side at the Santa Monica gym by the ocean. Sweat ran down his face and cheeks as he tried to finish his last rep. With wireless headphones in his ears, Johnny was giving this workout all he had. He shook and struggled to place the weight back on the bar. Once he was done, he turned and lifted his water bottle for a drink.

After he finished on the bench, Johnny made his way over to the shoulder press machine.

He added fifty pounds more weight, totaling one-hundred-fifty pounds. He took a few deep breaths, stretched his arms in both directions, and lifted up and down. After three sets of thirty reps, Johnny was getting very tired.

While on the shoulder press, Johnny noticed a man with a large neck and giant biceps walking toward him at a slow pace. He seemed awkward and out of place. Johnny could feel him staring. The man got closer and closer.

Johnny put the shoulder press down to lock it and looked over at the man who took the machine next to him.

"Can I help you?" Johnny asked as he became more paranoid.

"Do you mind if I ask...are you, Johnny Biggs? From the video?" the man said.

"Yeah, that's me," Johnny replied.

He then took a drink from his water bottle.

"Holy shit, I knew it. I saw you from across the gym. I couldn't believe it. In real life. Johnny Biggs."

"That's me. How can I help you?"

"I just wanted to say to you in person that what you did was amazing. Truly phenomenal. Can't believe I'm meeting you in the flesh. My name is Frank. Big fan," he said. "I was just wondering; would it be cool if I got a selfie with you?"

Johnny was stuck for a moment, not knowing how to respond. He had rarely ever been asked to take a picture with a fan before that knew he was not Cole.

"Umm, yeah, sure," Johnny said.

The muscular man stepped over to Johnny, pulled out his cell phone, opened the camera app, and snapped a few photos in selfie mode with Johnny standing next to him.

Frank grinned from ear to ear. He took a few more, and then shook Johnny's hand.

"Thank you, man," Frank said. "Means a lot to me. Got to meet Johnny Biggs in the flesh. Unreal."

Johnny laughed. "No worries at all."

"You know what? Would it be okay if I got an autograph?" Frank asked.

"Yeah, I suppose so," Johnny said. "What do you want me to sign?" He wiped the sweat from his forehead.

"Well, I got a marker right here," said Frank as he reached into his pocket and pulled out a permanent black marker. "How about you sign my phone?"

The man lifted up his smartphone wrapped in a golden phone case and handed it over to Johnny, followed by the black marker.

Johnny had never signed an autograph before, so at first, he wasn't sure how to sign his name. He decided to sign in cursive. "Johnny Biggs" he wrote on the back of the phone case. Johnny handed Frank his phone back.

"Here you go, man," he said.

"Thank you so much," said Frank. "It's an honor to meet you, Mister Biggs."

"Nice to meet you, too," Johnny replied.

The man walked away as he looked at Johnny's signature on his phone case.

Johnny picked up his water bottle and walked over to the chest press machine a few feet away.

The next morning, Johnny woke up thirty seconds before his alarm clock went off. He picked up his phone to see that it was 7:29 A.M.

Johnny rolled out of bed and began doing pushups on the hardwood floor. He dropped to the floor after fifty in a row and stretched his arms to the side and above his head.

That morning, Johnny took it upon himself to cook a little breakfast. Trevor was sleeping, but Johnny figured he would surprise him when he woke up.

Johnny cracked an egg on the side of a large green bowl. He ended up cracking an entire carton of eggs into the bowl and whisked them with a fork. He seasoned them with some pepper, garlic powder, and salt. He added a little bit of milk and mixed it all up. Johnny took two black non-stick frying pans and put them on the front and back burners. He turned the temperature up and threw a quarter butter stick on each.

On one of the pans, Johnny poured the mix of the dozen eggs, which swirled and covered the bottom of the pan. On the other pan, Johnny laid down about a pound of bacon, which began to sizzle in just a few moments. Then, he took a large wooden cooking spoon and mixed the eggs as they turned from liquid into a soft solid. The bacon slowly cooked on the bottom of the other pan. The smell floated from the pan in the kitchen, through the hallway, and into Trevor's room.

A few moments later, Johnny could hear Trevor shout from the other room, "Damn, that smells good!" A smile formed on Johnny's face. He continued to cook. He put four slices of white bread into the toaster.

Trevor came out of his bedroom a minute later. He was holding a blunt in one hand and a lighter in the other.

"Shit," Trevor said. "If you're making breakfast, I'll supply the weed. Ain't nothing better than blunts and breakfast!"

"Think it's a bit early for me, Trev," said Johnny before he flipped the bacon.

"Come on, live a little!" Trevor fired up the end of the blunt with his lighter. The ember turned orange as he inhaled the smoke. Trevor exhaled the smoke as a cloud drifted from the marijuana-filled cigar out through the kitchen. It hovered under the ceiling as it faded away into the air. Trevor took a few more puffs of the blunt before passing it over to his roommate.

Johnny rolled his eyes but placed the blunt between his lips. He took a big hit as his lungs and chest filled up with the powerful cannabis plant. Johnny let out a big exhale before coughing profusely.

55

Just then, the toast popped up out of the toaster. Johnny placed the slices on a small plate.

He coughed three more times.

"Bro, did it rain this morning?" Trevor asked.

"I think so," answered Johnny as he took another hit of the blunt.

Trevor looked out the window. His eyes widened when he noticed something spectacular.

"Yo dawg! There's a double fucking rainbow outside!" Trevor exclaimed.

"No way, really?" Johnny said as he put his giant wooden spoon down and took the frying pan containing the scrambled eggs off the stovetop.

"Yeah! Check it out!" Trevor shouted as a giant grin grew on his face.

Johnny looked outside the window and saw two rainbows perpendicular to one another in the distance. It was very vivid. He could see each color on each rainbow line separated from one another.

"Holy shit. That is sick!" Johnny said before puffing the thick marijuana cigar one more time. He then passed it back to Trevor. It must have been bigger than his thumb. The giant ember moved closer and closer to the mouthpiece as they continued to smoke. The two of them stood together and watched the double rainbow in amazement.

"I've never seen a double rainbow, bro," said Johnny.

"Same, my man," Trevor replied with the blunt in his mouth. Smoke was leaking from his nostrils. "Quite a sight."

"Indeed," Johnny nodded his head.

They watched the rainbows and smoked until the blunt was halfway gone.

Trevor put it out in the ash tray.

"Ugh, and to think I gotta work today, damn," Trevor said. "Smells good as hell, John. Can we eat?"

"Just a minute," Johnny replied as he turned off all the burners. He grabbed a couple of plates from the cupboard and put some eggs, toast and bacon on both dishes.

The two ate breakfast together as Trevor turned on some new music from one of his favorite rappers, Lil' Munny.

Later that day, Johnny was on the *Bullet Town 2* set filming a couple of extra stunts that they were adding for b roll.

Johnny was on a break, hanging out by the lunch catering table. He felt his phone vibrating in his pocket. He lifted it up to see a number that he did not recognize. After a few rings, he finally answered it.

"Hello?"

"Hey there, Johnny Biggs?" the voice said.

"Depends on who's calling," he replied.

"The name's Cashew. Cashew Peters," the man said. "I know you don't know me, but I got your number from my pal, Romeo Montana. He manages your boy, Cole," said Cashew.

"So, wait, your name's Cashew?" Johnny asked.

"That's what my momma named me," he said, laughing.

"That's nuts," Johnny said smirking.

"Ha, good one," the man replied.

"So, what can I do for you?"

"The real question would be, what can I do for you," Cashew replied.

"I'm not following," Johnny said.

"I want to be your agent," said Cashew.

"Huh? Agent?" Johnny said.

"Yeah. Your video is everywhere on the net. And I think with your background in stunts, and your newfound hero title, you could be a star. Better yet, a superstar. A real-life action hero superstar."

Johnny thought for a moment and said, "But I don't even act."

"It's not that hard. Trust me. Most of the stars these days can't either. But I want to get you on the big screen. Your face. Not just the side of you during a fight sequence. But your face on a poster," Cashew explained.

"Hmm. Really? You think I could act?" Johnny asked.

"I think it's worth a shot. Haven't you ever wanted to do more? To be more?"

Johnny thought to himself before he answered, "Perhaps I have."

"How about you meet me for dinner tonight? Hear me out a bit. Let me convince you why you should be a movie star," Cashew pleaded.

"Sure, I can do dinner. Why the hell not? I'll listen to what you have to say," said Johnny.

Later that night, after Johnny was done filming, he met Cashew Peters at The Cheesesteak Factory in downtown Los Angeles.

Cashew was a scrawny, rugged looking man in his early 30s with a thick orange beard. He wore a black suit and yellow tie with a white button-down shirt underneath. He had a strong Long Island accent. Johnny liked his attitude. He was funny, and convincing. He spent the entire night ordering drinks and food while explaining to Johnny why he thought that stuntman/hero Johnny Biggs would be a great fit for Hollywood.

"You would connect directly with the common man since you are one yourself. For now. But once people see a real man who can act and do his own stunts, they will be hooked. A fresh face for consumers to fall in love with on the big screen. So, what do you say? Will you let me be your agent? I will do my very best to make you a star" Cashew asked as he lifted his glass of expensive Merlot imported from Italy.

"Fuck it. Let's do it," said Johnny as he lifted his glass up as well.

They clinked their drinks together before they both finished what they had left on their plates.

"That's the spirit. It's all up from here, Johnny Biggs. You wait and see. To the moon!" Cashew shouted.

As they toasted, everyone in the restaurant was looking over at their table.

"To the moon," Johnny replied.

Chapter Eight

       Johnny was driving his Pompa SUV down River Street when he looked to the right and saw a man driving a large green truck texting and driving. The two came to a red light as Johnny pulled up beside the truck. Johnny rolled down his passenger-side window and shouted, "Quit driving while texting, ya jack ass!"

       The man looked to the left and saw Johnny. As soon as the light turned green, he flipped Johnny off with his middle finger and pressed on the gas to drive ahead. "Suit yourself, dumbass," he said to himself.

       Later that afternoon, Johnny was on the set filming more action scenes for the sequel of *Bullet Town*.

       Johnny traded strikes in the form of punches and kicks with Calvin. Calvin was an old friend of Johnny's. They had been doing stunt work together for several years.

       "Duck!" one of the stunt coordinators shouted. Johnny ducked, narrowly avoiding a big spinning heel kick from Calvin. Johnny then caught

Calvin with a swift uppercut directly to the jaw. Calvin dropped to the floor flat on his back.

Cole watched from the side, waiting patiently to alternate in between shots.

Johnny jumped just as Calvin went to sweep his legs. He followed the counter with a knee to the chest. Calvin backed up a little, then threw a big right hook that collided with Johnny's face. Johnny dropped to the ground.

"Cut!" yelled the videographer. "Let's swap Cole in for a few closeups. Then on to the big shooting sequence."

Cole walked to the marker where Johnny was lying. He reached down to pull Johnny to his feet.

"Thanks, man," said Johnny.

"Good shit, John," said Cole as he replaced Johnny on the ground.

Johnny walked to the side of one of the main video cameras. He felt his ribs. They were starting to sting. He may have hurt them during one of the falls in the fight scene. He landed sort of crooked after a kick.

He reached into his pocket, pulled out his prescription pill bottle, and unscrewed the cap quickly. He popped two pain pills in his mouth and watched as Cole read a few lines.

An hour later, Johnny was strapped to some high wires, hanging over the gritty prop street in Studio 17.

"Just one more take and I think we got it," said Chris, the videographer in charge that day. "Give us a few minutes and we'll shoot the final shot."

"No problem. I'll just hang out up here while we wait," said Johnny.

Vito, one of the other stuntmen in the film, laughed in his tuxedo attire.

When Johnny was finished shooting, he headed back to the locker room to get changed. He cracked open a cold can of Blizzard, a cherry carbonated energy drink. He guzzled it down. He was fairly tired from a long day of filming.

As Johnny was walking through the back of Studio 17, he bumped into Don Steiner, head producer of the *Bullet Town* trilogy.

"John!" Don said. "Just the man I was looking for."

"How can I help you, sir?" Johnny said. He was slightly confused as to why Don would want to speak to him.

"Yeah, your new agent reached out to me. Mister Cashew Peters," Don said.

"Okay, yeah, Cashew. Right. How'd that go?" Johnny asked.

"Well, he told me that you were interested in possibly acting. He said you were ready to do more than just stunt work," said Don.

"Well, sure, that is something I'm considering," Johnny replied.

"That's great to hear, John. By the way, I saw the video online of you saving that little girl. That was quite impressive," Don said.

"Why thank you, sir."

"So, when Cashew called and told me about his new client, I was intrigued to find he was talking about you. Had no idea you wanted to be a star, to be honest," Don said.

"Well, with all of this new publicity and a bit of convincing from Cashew, I figured why not give it a shot. It doesn't hurt to try, I suppose," said Johnny.

"Makes sense to me," said Don. "Well, once I got word that you would be acting…I had an idea. We got this new buddy cop movie in pre-production. It's called *Loose Ends*. I thought you would be great to audition for the role of 'Bruce'. How about you come in for an audition?"

Johnny took a swig of his energy drink. Then, he said, as calmly as possible, "I guess it wouldn't hurt to audition."

"That's the spirit," Don said, and patted Johnny on the back with force.

"I appreciate you guys thinking of me," Johnny said. He was flattered.

"I'll call the casting director and let him know you want to audition. How does Thursday sound?" Don asked.

"That should work. I'm off from filming that day," Johnny said.

"Yes, I know," said Don as he began to laugh. "Okay, bud. Catch up soon."

Don walked back the other way. Johnny headed into the locker room.

Johnny went home after work. He pulled up to his house and parked the Pompa in the driveway. He took the keys out of the ignition and exited the vehicle.

He walked inside to an empty house. It was quiet. You could usually hear music blasting through the speakers from outside. But not a peep. Trevor was still at work.

Johnny walked through the living room, down the hall and into his bedroom. He kicked his shoes off and dropped on his back on his queen-sized mattress. He was extremely tired. He had been shooting all day. And on top of all his other stunts, he'd had one very strenuous stunt where he was pulled through the window of a moving car. He landed on a crash pad, but he'd bounced off, rolling on the hard ground and bashing his elbow. But the pain was nothing he couldn't handle. His elbow was just a bit swollen. It looked like a tennis ball.

Then Johnny watched a bunch of videos online. He studied famous scenes and monologues from various films and television.

Later that day, Johnny got a call from Carl, one of the casting directors for *Loose Ends*. They set up an audition for Thursday afternoon.

After the call, Johnny closed his eyes and fell into a nap state. He began to dream. It was only 6:45 in the evening.

About an hour later, Johnny woke up as a cloud of smoke bathed him and floated into his nostrils. Trevor was standing over him, blowing smoke from a blunt into Johnny's face while he was sleeping. Johnny began to cough.

"What the hell?" said Johnny. The marijuana began to take effect before he could even rub his eyes.

"Get up! It's sushi night, bro," said Trevor as he puffed on the blunt some more.

"Ugh," said Johnny. "I'm tired, my G."

"Too tired for sushi? Who are you? My best friend, John, would never say that about sushi," said Trevor.

"Okay, fine. You're right. I told you, sushi tonight. That's what we're doing. Let me get dressed and ready. Gimme ten mins," said Johnny as he sat up from his bed.

"Sounds good, I'll go play a quick round of *League of Shooters*. Let me know when you're ready to bounce," said Trevor.

"For sure," Johnny replied.

After a fifteen-minute drive, Johnny and Trevor arrived at Mount Fuji, their favorite sushi spot in town. Trevor was playing rap music through the subwoofers at maximum volume. Trevor pulled the Pompa into the back parking lot, found a spot, and parked the car. The two got out, walked around from the back, and went inside through the front.

"Reservation for Trev," he said to the restaurant host.

"Ah, yes. Right this way," the host said after he analyzed his guest list. He grabbed a couple of menus and led Johnny and Trevor to their booth near the back of the restaurant. They sat down at their table as a young waiter approached them.

"Welcome to Mount Fuji. Can I get you something to drink?" the waiter asked.

"Can we get two orders of the large saké, as well as some ice waters?" asked Trevor.

"Of course," said the waiter. "Coming right up. And our special rolls for tonight are the Dancing Eel Roll and the Dynamite Shrimp Roll."

"Ah, that sounds good actually," said Johnny.

"Very good," said the waiter who nodded his head before heading to the kitchen to get their drinks.

The place had a very authentic Japanese feel to it. Classical Japanese music played in the background, creating a calm aura in the restaurant.

The waiter brought them two waters and warm bottles of saké, as well as two tiny cups to go with the saké.

"What can I get you?" asked the waiter as he pulled out his little yellow notepad and a pen.

Trevor ordered a large sashimi boat for the table that included a fresh raw fish assortment arranged in a very artistic fashion. He placed an order for pork gyoza and crab Rangoon. They both ordered a couple of spider rolls and dragon rolls for their entrees.

After the waiter took their order, Trevor scrolled through his MyFace feed.

"Dude, did I tell you? I got an agent," Johnny blurted out.

"Wait, what?" Trevor asked as he looked up from his phone.

"Yeah, Cashew Peters. He's actually pretty legit. I guess they want me to audition for a movie or something," said Johnny.

"Bro, that's amazing!" Trevor exclaimed.

"Yeah. But I don't know. I'm having second thoughts. A few doubts in my mind, I suppose," Johnny said.

"What do you mean? What kind of doubts?"

"I don't know. What if I suck ass? I've never really had to say anything. Just did my stunts and that's it."

Trevor poured some saké from the bottle and into both cups. He handed one to Johnny.

"Nah, bro. This is your moment. Do you know how long I wanted you to do this? Plus, now the internet sees you as a real-life hero. Might as well get paid to play one on the big screen. Aren't you sick of doing all the hard work just so someone else gets the credit?" Trevor asked.

Johnny thought about it for a second as he scratched his chin.

"I guess you have a point."

Trevor lifted his cup and said, "Here's a toast. Here's to the first day of the rest of your life!"

"Cheers!" Johnny clinked his cup against Trevor's before they both chugged down the warm saké.

66

"That's my man!"

"But, Trev, it's like, I don't even know how to act. I guess I gotta start practicing. They're sending me the script for the audition soon."

"Bro, how hard can it be?" Trevor asked.

"I guess we'll see," Johnny responded.

Just then, their waiter brought over a tray with their crab Rangoon puffs and pork gyoza dumplings. He placed their appetizers on the table and walked away.

Chapter Nine

Johnny wandered around the house with his phone in his hand. He opened his email and clicked on a file which began downloading to his phone. Then he opened the file. The top of the page read, *Loose Ends*.

He paced back and forth in the living room, reading the script. Johnny had never really read the words of the scripts he was given in the past because he never had too many lines to speak. He was always focused on the stunts because that's what he did. He was now stepping out of his comfort zone just by reading the words in the script.

He read for a minute, trying to envision the voice of the character he would be playing. He walked to the kitchen, opened the refrigerator, and pulled out a bottle of Crow Light, his favorite beer. He twisted the top off and guzzled it down as the foam surfaced to the top of the bottle.

The front door was suddenly kicked open as Trevor walked inside. "Johnny! My man!"

"What's going on, Trev?"

Johnny took another swig of beer. He placed his phone on the kitchen counter.

Trevor gave him a high five.

"Just coolin.' Glad to be home."

Trevor opened the fridge and grabbed a Crow Light bottle as well. "What you up to?"

"I'm just reading this script they sent me," said Johnny.

"Hell yeah, that's my boy! How is it so far?"

"I'm still on the first couple of pages, but I guess it's pretty good so far."

Just then, Johnny's phone started going off. It rang and rang. Johnny looked at the Home Screen and saw that it was Cole calling.

"Hold up. I gotta take this," he said as he picked up the phone.

"Yo, Cole," said Johnny as he walked down the hall and into his bedroom.

"Johnny Biggs, my main man, how the fuck are you doing?"

"I'm good, Cole. Real good. How about you?"

"I'm great, brother. As always. Wanted to hit you up. Just got an offer for this movie called *Mummy Zombies*. Figured I'd reach out and make sure you're available," said Cole.

"Well, actually, I suppose it depends on when we start shooting."

"Oh. Hmm. Well, I believe it starts in December."

"Hmm. I guess I have to see how this other thing goes," Johnny replied.

"What other thing?"

"Don Steiner asked me to audition for an upcoming role."

"No shit. Really?" Cole asked. "You're gonna like, act? Or is it for stunt work?"

"They want me to give acting a shot. Don says I would be great for the role."

"Wow, I didn't know you were contemplating switching from stunts," said Cole.

"I'm not switching permanently or anything, just figured I would at least give it a try. What could it hurt?"

"Well, our schedule for one," said Cole.

"You mean your schedule."

"Well, my schedule is our schedule, Johnny. You're my stunt double. I need you on call at all times," said Cole, his voice getting more serious as the call went on.

"I'm not even sure if it's gonna happen. It's quite a long shot, man. They just want me to come in. I'm sure I'll be able to still do stunts for you," Johnny explained.

"As much as I want to see you shine, I need you. I don't want to have to find another double," Cole said.

"You won't. You know I'm loyal. Always have been, always will be. Plus, I doubt I'll even get the part. My acting is shit. Never even really tried."

"My best advice. Stick to what you know. You may be a great actor, who knows? But do you know how many great actors and actresses get overlooked and never even get a chance on the big screen? Thousands upon thousands. You already have a spot as a stuntman, and not just any stuntman. My stuntman. And I wouldn't mess that up for anything. Just my personal opinion," Cole went on.

"Don't worry, Cole. Again, I doubt it's going to lead to anything. But when Don mentioned it, I figured it was in my best interest to go with the flow."

"I get it. You said you've never acted before, right?" asked Cole.

"Nah, just my stunts for the most part," Johnny responded.

"It ain't easy. You're gonna forget lines, you're gonna get frustrated with the directors and other actors. It ain't easy, I can tell you that. But, hey, give it a shot."

"You think I may be decent at least?" Johnny asked.

"I'm gonna be honest with you. I don't see it happening. You're a great stuntman, Johnny. Really. The best. But if you haven't figured out how to act by now, I don't really see it in your future. Not to be an asshole or anything. You're really good...at making me look good. Together, we are amazing. I just hope you don't fail miserably. I've seen it happen far too many times to count," said Cole.

Johnny was starting to get annoyed with Cole's discouraging comments.

"You know what? I guess we'll just have to see how it goes," said Johnny, trying to conceal his irritation. "Don sees something in me, so that's good enough for me."

"Don sees something in *everyone*. Especially the actresses he hires. I'm sure you've heard about Dirty Don and all the bullshit he pulls."

"Nah, not really. What do you mean?"

"Let's just say, Don Steiner is the biggest creep in Hollywood. That's all I'll say about that for now."

Johnny started to get the feeling that Cole was jealous of Don and even resentful about the new attention Johnny was getting. He brushed Cole's comments off and said, "Okay, thanks for the heads up."

"Johnny, I gotta run. Just wanted to check in with you. Oh yeah, also wanted to invite you to my big birthday bash next weekend. I'll send you the deets. It's at Bulb Nightclub downtown."

"Wouldn't miss it for the world," Johnny replied.

"Awesome. All right, talk to you soon. Remember, Johnny, December, *Mummy Zombies*. I need you," said Cole.

"I'll keep you posted, brother. I should be all good to go."

"Sounds good. Talk to you soon, Biggs," said Cole.

"Later," said Johnny as he hung up the call.

Johnny walked out of his bedroom and into the hallway. He closed the door behind him. He pulled out his phone, opened up the script file, and began to read some more.

"Everything all right?" asked Trevor who was sitting on the couch with a bag of cheese puffs to his side.

"Yeah, bro. That was just Cole. Told him about my upcoming audition," said Johnny.

"Oh snap. I can't believe you told him about it! And how did he react?" Trevor took a drink from his bottle of beer.

"Not too great. I don't think he wants me doing it," said Johnny.

"I mean, it makes sense. You are his boy, ya know what I mean? Probably doesn't want to lose his go-to guy, his stunt double," said Trevor as he reached into his snack bag and took out a handful of cheese puffs.

"Honestly, it kind of motivated me even more to knock this shit out of the park. Fuck it. I'm going to get this role," Johnny said with authority.

Later that night, Johnny stared at himself in the hallway mirror. He had his phone in hand, with the *Loose Ends* script lit up on the screen.

"*What makes you think you should be on this side of town?*" Johnny said aloud.

He repeated the question one more time, while looking at the screen, making sure he was reading it correctly. "*What makes you think...that you should be on this side of town?*"

He made a few different faces, trying to figure out the right expression to go with the line. At first, he made a confused face, before switching to an angry face.

He scrolled down to read more of the script.

Johnny got to page two and tried reading some more of the lines.

"*Who do you think you are!*" Johnny shouted at himself in the mirror. He pointed at himself as he squinted his left eye.

"*I told you today was not the day to come to me with this bullshit,*" Johnny said. "*No, I told you. Today is really not the day to come at me with this bullshit!*"

He paced back and forth, working on his walk. He was not entirely sure how his character was supposed to look. He felt awkward trying to walk like a tough guy, but slowly figured out a smoother variation that seemed like a more natural fit.

"That's more like it," Johnny said as he strutted through his living room.

Chapter Ten

Johnny was off from work for the next couple of weeks until his following stunt gig. He had been reading the script for *Loose Ends* non-stop. He stayed up until four in the morning more than once trying to find the right tone to use for his character. He was trying out for the part of a guy named "Bruce" the lead role in an action movie that revolved around a man looking to avenge the death of his wife and children.

The night before his audition, Trevor convinced Johnny to go out to their favorite local bar, Tino's. They pre-gamed at the house with a bottle of Frank Thompson whiskey. By that time, Johnny had had about four shots, while Trevor had beat him with six.

It was a cloudy and gray Wednesday night, and the air was very thick.

As the clock struck nine, Johnny and Trevor chatted away, laughing, and pounding shots. Once they were both nice and tipsy, the two took a taxi downtown to Tino's. They met up with their buddies, Dan and Barney, who were waiting there with two pitchers of beer. Barney was the hefty one of the crew, while Dan was the short one. They sat at a table in the rear of the packed hole-in-the-wall bar further away from the crowd.

"Johnny, when's that new movie with Cole coming out?" Dan asked.

"Honestly, Danny, I don't really know. I think a few months from now. I know they're in post-production," Johnny replied.

"Word. I loved the last one. Just watched it with my girl last night. I was even able to point out the parts you were in. She couldn't believe it. I was friends with a movie star who is friends with Cole Tillman," Dan said.

"Thanks, bro," said Johnny sarcastically.

"Actually, Biggs might be starring in his own movie soon," Trevor blurted out.

"What?" said Barney. "No way!"

"Yeah, I'm keeping it under wraps for now. Not really telling anyone, Trev!"

"He's got an audition tomorrow!" Trevor shouted.

"Here's to Johnny!" Dan said as he lifted his beer for a toast. The rest of the squad joined in and clinked their mugs together.

"To Johnny!" Barney and Trevor said in unison. They all drank from their mugs. Loud rap music blared even louder through the speakers.

While the guys talked together and began to catch up, Johnny noticed a man staring at him from the bar. The man was wearing a pinstriped suit, and a black button-down underneath. The man glared at Johnny for a few seconds before he looked away and got on his phone. Johnny did not think much of it at first. He picked up his mug of beer and took a swig.

The night went on, and the boys were all partying, having a great time. Johnny went to the bar to order a round for the table.

"How about some shots?" said Johnny as he returned with the four shot glasses filled to the top with tequila. He'd begun to loosen up a bit. He almost forgot about his audition the next afternoon. However, it was still in the back of his mind. He knew he would have to go home at some point if he wanted to get any sleep before the big day.

"You're the man!" Dan shouted.

The four of them took their shots. Trevor shouted out, "Fuck yeah!"

"It's good to have the boys back together," said Barney.

Later that night, a group of lively women approached Johnny and his friends. One of them introduced herself as Pam.

"These are my friends Tory, Monica, and Lori. We figured you guys could use some company," said Pam.

"Nice to meet you ladies," said Trevor as he shook hands and introduced himself. "My name is Trevor."

"Do you mind me asking…are you, Cole Tillman?" Tory asked Johnny.

"Actually, it's the next best thing. That's Cole's stuntman, Johnny," said Barney. "I'm Barney. And this is Dan," he said while pointing to his friend.

The girls all looked at each other for a moment. Then, Pam said, "That's okay. Still very impressive!"

The girls grabbed some seats and hung out with the guys for a while. They danced as a group casually. Then Monica asked Johnny if he would like to dance. He was getting drunker as the night went on. He agreed and danced with her to the hit radio song, "Last Night" by Krista Cooper.

"I love this song!" she yelled at Johnny who could barely hear her over the loud music.

When the song was almost finished, Monica was jumping around from side to side and accidentally spilled her drink all over Johnny's white button shirt.

"Oh my gosh! I'm soooo sorry!" she shouted. Monica grabbed a napkin from the table and tried to clean him off.

"It's okay. No worries at all," Johnny said.

"Let me make it up to you," she said as she pulled him down closer to her and gave him a big kiss.

"Wow!" Pam said. "You go girl!"

Johnny kissed Monica for about five seconds before she stepped back.

He didn't know what to say at first. He looked down at her drink and said, "Looks like you need another drink. I'll go grab us some at the bar."

"Sounds great, handsome!" she replied.

Johnny made his way through the packed crowd and over to the bar. There was a long line and only three bartenders on duty.

Johnny waited behind a few men who were ordering drinks. He got closer to the front of the line. He looked to his right and noticed the man in the pin-striped suit was still staring at him.

"Why have you been grilling me all night?!" Johnny shouted toward the man.

The man ignored him, turned around, picked up his phone, and walked outside the bar.

"Fucking weirdo," Johnny said to himself.

He got to the front of the line.

"What are you having?" the bartender asked.

"I'll take your best draft beer," Johnny slurred. "Oh, and one Long Island iced tea, please and thank you."

"Coming right up," the bartender said.

Johnny waited for his drinks. While waiting, he listened to two men next to him debate what stocks they should buy the next morning. Johnny rolled his eyes.

The bartender handed Johnny the drinks and said, "That will be $22.50."

Johnny handed him a twenty-dollar bill and a ten-dollar bill. "Keep the change," said Johnny.

He looked over toward the entrance of the bar and saw the same man in the pinstriped suit come back inside. This time he was followed by four other men in suits. The man in the pinstriped suit walked toward Johnny.

"Cole Tillman?"

"Huh?" Johnny replied.

"Mister Tillman, we need to talk to you," the man said.

"I'm sorry, you have the wrong person," said Johnny. "That's not me."

"Mister Tillman, Mister Martino has been very patient with you and your debts. But we have been sent here to collect at least half of what you owe our boss."

"Buddy, I have no fucking clue what you are talking about," said Johnny.

"Cole, Mister Martino expects his money tonight. We can either do this the easy way or the hard way, movie star," said the young mobster.

"Listen, you better get the hell out of my face right now, buddy," said Johnny as he backed up a bit with the drinks in his hands.

"You mean to tell me you don't have the money? Again?" the man said in an angrier, louder voice and tone.

"How many times I gotta tell you? I'm not Cole Tillman!"

"Looks like him to me, Richie," said the guy standing behind the man in the pinstriped suit. Johnny saw that the guy must have been at least six-foot-four. He was built like a football linebacker. Johnny felt like he could take on the rest of them, but he was not sure about that one.

"I agree, Tony. I agree," said Richie. "It's gotta be him."

Johnny's friends noticed the disturbance by the bar.

"Oh shit. What's going on with Johnny?" asked Trevor as he saw the guys confronting him.

"Look, whatever beef you got with Cole. That isn't me. That's my good friend, however. And I doubt he would owe you dumb goofy goons anything. He's loaded!"

"Sir, you owe Mister Martino $400,000! We've given you enough time," said Richie.

"What? Four hundred…man, get the hell out of here," said Johnny.

"Screw this," said the linebacker, Tony, as he lunged through the crowd and toward Johnny.

Johnny instinctively backed away, cocked back, and bashed the large mobster with both the mug and glass cup. The glass cup shattered over his head. The bar crowd began screaming and hollering.

Johnny's friends left the girls and ran over immediately. The other goons were going for Johnny. Johnny hopped up on the bar counter. Richie reached for his legs. Johnny jumped up, dodging Richie. He then kicked him in the face, making him spit blood all over his pinstriped suit.

Just then, another man in a black suit swept Johnny's legs out from under him making him crash down onto the countertop. The wooden surface cracked as Johnny landed flat. He made sure to tuck his head, even in his current state of inebriation.

Trevor saw Richie cocking back to blast Johnny who was laying on his back. Trevor caught his arm, making Richie turn around with a big back elbow to his face. Trevor dropped to the ground. Barney ran over and tackled Richie into a bar stool. Both men went flying to the ground.

Johnny kicked up, propelling himself off the counter and onto his feet. Another man turned Johnny around before punching him in the eye. Johnny took one more before dodging the third punch and uppercutting the goon in the jaw. The man went flying after flipping behind the bar.

Patrons scattered out of fear for their lives while some guys surrounded the men in a circle, cheering, and chanting, "Fight! Fight! Fight!" Most of the girls were screaming.

Tony went charging at Johnny. Just before he got to him, Johnny placed his foot on the countertop and backflipped. While he soared into the air, Tony turned around to find Johnny's foot kicking him across the cheek. The big man stumbled back into the crowd. It was complete and utter chaos.

Johnny looked around to see his friends having his back and joining in on the brawl. It felt like slow motion as a bottle of beer went flying into the air upside down before his eyes. He watched as the beer came out of the bottle and poured all over a woman's head drenching her and her dress.

Johnny ran over and did a flying donkey kick to the chest of the goon who was beating on Dan. Johnny turned around and was met with a bar stool to the side of his head. One of the goons cracked it in half very close to Johnny's skull.

Johnny fell to the ground for a moment. Then he stood back up, lifted the man in the air, and dropped him on his upper shoulders. The guy smacked his head on the table before hitting the ground.

Johnny looked around and noticed a few people in the crowd were filming the altercation in progress.

The girls that were hanging out with the squad stayed to watch the guys brawling with the mobsters.

"Wow, they're so tough," said Pam.

"You don't need another tough guy, Pamela," said Monica. "You need a nice guy."

"I don't know. Johnny seems pretty nice, too," said Pam. Just then, Johnny jumped up and did a spinning heel kick to the side of Richie's head, dropping him to the ground.

"We gotta get out of here," Johnny said to Trevor. Dan and Barney overheard it. They each punched the attackers in the face.

The group scurried through the crowd and out the front door. Pam shouted, "Call me!" She then blew a kiss to Johnny.

Once outside, Johnny and his crew took off running down the street. Johnny was not sure if more guys would show up to fight them. He was bleeding slightly from the left eye and his right eye was already turning black and blue. Barney's jaw was cut open and Trevor had a black eye.

After a couple of minutes of running and silence, they slowed to a walk. No one made a noise until Trevor broke the silence by saying, "That was…fucking awesome!"

"Hell yeah! We kicked their ass!" Barney shouted.

Johnny smiled, then realized his eye was swelling up when he caught a glimpse of himself in the reflection of a car window.

"Shit, I have my audition tomorrow," he said out loud.

"Don't worry. It doesn't look that bad," said Trevor. "You'll be fine."

Chapter Eleven

Johnny paced around the waiting room lobby of the Wilson casting studio just a few blocks down from Hollywood Boulevard. He had been waiting for fifteen minutes to be called into the room with the casting directors and producers for the upcoming film *Loose Ends.*

About a dozen other men sat in chairs around the large lobby waiting for their turns as well. Most of them looked eerily similar to Johnny. Johnny even recognized a couple of them from various commercials and different movie gigs he'd worked on. Others had been extras or played supporting roles in some of the movies he did stunts for.

Johnny made eye contact with one of the actors who seemed to be going over his lines. He gave him a head nod and the actor nodded back. The actor had a similar hairstyle to Johnny's, wavy and thin.

While he was waiting, Johnny got a text from Trevor. He noticed in his notifications that it was a link to a video. Johnny clicked on it. It was a video of the bar fight. His eyes opened wide. He couldn't believe the video already had over 150,000 views.

Johnny texted Trevor back, "What the hell!"

"I know, right! Don't I look like a badass? We're internet famous!" Trevor texted back.

"Audition starting soon. Talk to you later," Johnny typed before shutting off his phone and putting it in his pocket.

One of the production assistants came out of the conference room and said, "Johnny Biggs, we're ready for you."

"That's me," said Johnny.

He took a deep breath before following the man into the room.

Johnny walked through the door and was greeted by a half dozen people. Four men and two women. They were either casting directors or producers.

"Okay, Johnny. Nice to meet you. We are very excited about your audition. We will begin with scene four in Act Two. Ready whenever you are," said Tim, one of the film's producers. Johnny stretched for a second and nodded his head. He took another deep breath.

Johnny read the first line he remembered from the script. *"Man, you must be the captain of cappin' with your lying ass. Don't come around here feeding me that bullshit!"*

The whole room stared in astonishment. Johnny was really selling the role. They couldn't see his palms beginning to sweat from nervousness.

One of the producers read the other lines that went with the scene.

"Why would I need to lie to you?"

"Because that's what you do. You lie," Johnny said as an angry look grew on his face.

"Who the hell do you think you are?" the producer yelled from his casting chair.

84

"I think I'm the last person you'll ever see again if you don't tell me where they are."

"I already told you. I don't know where they are!"

"You're really starting to piss me off. You know how I get when I'm pissed, right?" asked Johnny.

"I'm not trying to upset you," the producer read.

"Well, it appears you don't even have to try. I'm beyond upset," said Johnny. His face grew redder as the scene went on.

Johnny stared at the group of casting directors and producers. He made an angry face followed by a blank stare. The directors were eating it up.

"Look at that black and blue eye makeup, he's so committed to the role," one of the producers whispered to his colleague.

"I don't care what you told me. I know you know something," Johnny read from the script.

"Listen. If you want to find them. You need to speak to Sal. He's the only one I know that may know," the producer read.

"If I find out that you knew where they were but didn't tell me, I'm going to come back here with a bat...and bash your damn brains in," Johnny said with a mean glare.

"And end scene," said Robin, the head casting director.

Johnny took a deep breath when he realized it was over.

"Very good," she said. "You ooze vulnerability."

"I agree," said Tim.

"We love your look, too. You really committed to the role with black eye makeup, cuts and bruises," said Robin.

"Oh no, this is actually real," Johnny said while pointing to his eye which was swollen purple.

There was a brief moment of silence before the directors and producers burst out laughing.

Johnny knew he was being serious, but their laughter was a good sign regardless.

"We got a special request from Don Steiner to have you audition. So that is always a good sign. We will be in touch," said Robin.

She walked over and shook Johnny's hand. "Great job."

"Thank you," he said.

He shook hands with everyone in the room before he walked out the door.

Later that night, Johnny was back at home heating up his frozen barbecue rib meal. It had two minutes left in the microwave. The moonlight began to pierce through the windows of Johnny's townhouse.

Johnny was scrolling his MyFace feed. He came across an article about a famous rock star, Todd Conrad, who changed his life around from being addicted to drugs and alcohol to five years of sobriety. It reminded Johnny to medicate himself. He reached into his pocket and pulled out his bottle of prescription painkillers. He unscrewed the cap and popped two into his mouth.

Johnny continued to read the article. He was a big fan of Todd Conrad's music. The article inspired him. He felt like one day he would be able to wean himself off of his painkiller medication. But his constant state of pain made him rely on the pills to function.

The microwave beeped. Johnny went over, opened it up, and took out his piping hot barbecue rib frozen dinner. He peeled the cellophane off of the box before mixing up the food with a fork. The ribs came with a side of mashed potatoes and macaroni and cheese.

Johnny sat down in a chair next to the dining table with his food, a fork, and an ice-cold bottle of beer. He searched for some of Todd Conrad's music on StreamHub, his go-to music streaming service. He played the song, "Let it Ride" and turned up the volume. Once he placed his phone on the table, he began to eat.

After a few minutes, the song stopped playing as the phone rang and vibrated.

Johnny looked at the Caller ID, then picked up and said, "What's up, Cole?"

"Johnny! How's it hanging?" Cole asked.

"Oh, you know, same shit, different day," Johnny replied. "How are you?"

"I'm all right, Johnny. Living day to day," said Cole.

"Hey, I didn't want to bother you, but something happened the other night while we were out at the bar. It was really weird, actually," said Johnny.

"What happened?" Cole asked.

"Well, I was out with my boys at the bar having a good time. And out of nowhere these guys approached me. They thought I was you. They started harassing me about some debts I guess you owed their boss," Johnny explained.

"No fucking way, damn," Cole replied.

"Yeah, we ended up getting into this big bar room brawl. After a while, we left before the cops showed up. Shit was pretty crazy. Some people even videotaped it and put it online. Getting a lot of views, actually."

"Wow. I'm sorry, John. Well, cool about the views. But. I never meant for you to get caught up in my shit. You okay? They hurt you?" Cole asked.

"I'm all right. A couple scratches, no big deal," Johnny said.

"That's terrible. Sorry to hear that. Sorry to hear that happened. I've been working on paying them," said Cole.

"What the hell happened? You got money," Johnny said.

"I do and I don't. Most of my money is tied up somewhere. I'm actually in debt quite a bit, as embarrassing as it is to admit. All I have are my assets. May have to start selling some cars. I've owed these guys money for a while now. A couple of bad bets went south. Long story short, I don't have their money," Cole explained.

"Bruh, how do you not have any savings, even an emergency fund?" Johnny asked.

"Easier said than done, John. When you live like I live, it requires a certain lifestyle," Cole said.

"You need a financial consultant or someone to take care of your money. You had a number one movie last year," said Johnny.

"You're right. And WE had a number one movie. And we will again! But again, I'm sorry," Cole said.

"It's all right. Not the first time I've taken a punch for you," Johnny said before laughing.

"You're a good man, John. This won't happen again," said Cole.

Just then, a call came in on the other line. It was Johnny's new agent, Cashew Peters.

"Hey Cole, listen. I have another call coming in I have to take. Can we finish this conversation later?"

"Yeah, of course. Call me later," said Cole.

"Will do," said Johnny before he ended the call and answered the other.

"Hello?" Johnny said.

"Mister Biggs! It's Cashew. Got some great news!"

"Oh cool, what's that?" Johnny asked as he took a bite into his barbecue ribs now that they were cooled down.

"You got the part! You're going to be starring in *Loose Ends*!"

"You're shitting me," Johnny replied. His heart began to race. A smile appeared on his face.

"I shit you not," said Cashew. "Time to make you a superstar!"

Chapter Twelve

A month went by, and Johnny spent the majority of his time memorizing the script for *Loose Ends*. The studio even set him up with an acting coach, just to make sure he was fully prepared for the role. Johnny got along well with his coach, Dylan. He was a great teacher, and conditioned Johnny for the part.

On a Monday morning, Johnny pulled up to the *Loose Ends* production set in his Pompa SUV. He drove around back and found a parking spot in the actors' parking lot. The sun shone bright, and the Hollywood air was fairly thick and humid that day.

Johnny put the large car into park, took the key from the ignition, and gathered his things. He took out his bottle of prescription medication and popped two pills to help calm his nerves and soothe his back pain.

He got out of his car, slung his duffel bag onto his shoulder, locked the door, and walked toward the rear entrance to studio Lot 23.

Johnny walked down a long dark hallway. There was no one in sight. After a minute of searching,

Johnny was approached by a production assistant holding a clipboard.

"Mister Biggs, you can get changed in your trailer out back," the young man said.

"My trailer?" Johnny asked.

"Yes, sir. I can show you there," the man said. "My name is Rudy, nice to meet you. It's an honor to work with you!"

"Pleasure to meet you, Rudy," said Johnny before shaking his hand.

Johnny followed Rudy out of the building and toward the trailers for the actors and actresses.

He was led to his rather large silver trailer. Johnny could not believe it. He was so used to changing in locker rooms or with the other stuntmen. He never imagined he would have his own trailer. He noticed that the sign on the door read "Johnny Biggs" with two stars on both sides of his name.

"We will come get you when it's time to shoot your first scene, Mister Biggs," said Rudy. "Is there anything you need in the meantime?"

"I would love a soda, actually," said Johnny.

"No problem. What flavor?"

"How about an orange soda?" Johnny said.

"Sure thing, coming right up."

Johnny stepped inside his trailer. "Damn, this is fucking sweet," he said to himself.

He dropped his black duffel bag in the middle of the trailer and looked around. He saw there was a leather couch, a table and chair, bathroom, and even a tiny kitchen with a fridge and sink.

He walked over to his refrigerator and opened it. He found all sorts of products in there, including a tray with pre-made sandwiches. He helped himself to one stuffed with roast beef. "Damn, that's not half bad." He took another bite and went back to the couch to settle in and kick his feet up.

"This is the life," he said to himself.

He reached into his duffel bag and pulled out the *Loose Ends* script. He figured that he would read it one more time to prepare for the day's scenes.

A few minutes went by before Johnny heard a knock on the door.

"Just a minute!" he said as he finished the last couple bites of his sandwich and put down the script. Johnny walked over to open the trailer door.

"Sir, we are going to need you for makeup in twenty minutes," Rudy said. "And here's your orange soda."

"Oh, okay. Thanks, that's cool. Where do I go for makeup?"

"Down that way, turn right and down the hallway of Studio 18."

"Hmm, all right. I'm sure I'll find it," said Johnny.

"We'll send somebody to bring you there," Rudy told him.

"Sounds good," Johnny said.

"You enjoying your new trailer, Mister Biggs?"

"I sure am. This is great."

"Glad to hear," said Rudy before shutting the door and walking away.

Twenty minutes later, another knock was heard at the door. Johnny exited his trailer and followed one of the production assistants through the lot and down the studio halls, where they finally reached the makeup artist's room.

Johnny knocked on the door where the sign read, "Makeup."

A woman opened the door. Johnny was surprised by how beautiful she was.

"Johnny! Nice to finally meet you," she said as she approached him with a hug and a kiss on the cheek. "My name is Gloria. I will be doing your makeup for the film."

"Nice to meet you, Gloria," Johnny said as he began to blush. She had long brown and blonde hair. She was wearing a lime green dress. Johnny could not stop admiring her curves, but he veered his eyes toward hers to remain respectful.

"Come on in. Take a seat," said Gloria.

The production assistant walked away as Johnny followed Gloria inside the room. He took a seat on a chair.

"So, I'm just going to give you a little bit of color, and maybe hide a few of these beautiful scars you got," Gloria said.

"All right. Just don't make me too pretty now," Johnny said before laughing.

Gloria laughed as well.

She touched up the marks on his face with some blush. Johnny could not help but admire her beauty. Gloria was not oblivious to this.

"So, I hear this is the first movie that you're starring in," she said.

"That is correct," Johnny replied. "I've done lots of stunt work over the years. This is actually my first speaking role, really."

"Wow, you must be pretty good if they made you the lead," Gloria said.

"Well, I'm not gonna toot my own horn or nothing. But yeah, I guess they liked me," Johnny said.

"I just hope one day I can be as lucky," Gloria said as she applied some powder to his cheeks. "I'm an actress, you know."

"For real? I mean, I believe it."

"Yeah, I am. Just haven't really gotten too many opportunities just yet."

"Hmm. You're absolutely gorgeous. I'm sure you'll make it one day," said Johnny.

Gloria turned bright red and said in a very flirtatious tone, "Stop it, Johnny!"

"What? It's true. You're absolutely stunning if you ask me," he said.

"Stop making me blush!" She walked away so he could not see her face.

"How's your acting?" Johnny asked.

"Pretty damn good," Gloria said as she walked back over.

Johnny thought to himself for a moment before he said, "Maybe I can get you a role in my next movie if this one goes well."

"Quit playing with me. You're just saying that."

"Nah, for real. If all goes according to plan, and they want me for another one...I'll make sure to get you a role."

"Don't you build me up now just to hurt me later," she said as a smile began to form on her face.

"I'm serious," he said. That's when the two of them locked eyes for a moment.

"I'm gonna hold you to that, Johnny," said Gloria.

She finished his makeup and began working on his hair. She used some moisturizing products to make his hair appear thicker and wavier. She then flipped the front of his hair up and styled it a bit.

"All right. You're done for the day. Looking very handsome if I do say so myself," Gloria said.

"Thank you, hun," Johnny replied.

He turned around to look at himself in the mirror. "Whoa. I look brand new."

On his way out of the room, Johnny turned around and said, "For real, though. If I can, I will get you in a movie. Maybe we can be costars on my next one."

"Let's make sure you do good this time. And I'll believe it when I see it," Gloria said. She gave him a hug and a kiss on the cheek. "Now I believe they need you in wardrobe to get you suited up in your costume."

"Sounds good, think you can walk me there?" Johnny asked with a smile.

"Sure, why not?" Gloria replied. The two walked together down the hallway.

Later, Johnny found his trailer and let himself inside the air-conditioned room. He sat on the couch. Another orange soda was on the nearby coffee table next to a small bucket of ice.

Johnny picked up his script and read the scenes for the day over and over again. He only had to shoot two that day. But he wanted to make sure he was as prepared as he could be.

The clock struck one. Johnny fell asleep on the couch while reading the script. A loud banging on the trailer door woke Johnny up from his nap.

"Huh? What's up?" Johnny said as he came to and realized he had been sleeping. "Oh shit, coming!"

Johnny took a deep breath before he opened his trailer door and walked outside.

"This way, Mister Biggs. You are needed on set for filming," the assistant told him.

"Let's fucking do this," Johnny said.

He then proceeded to crack his knuckles as he followed the assistant to the set.

On the way, Johnny walked by a door that read "Don Steiner." As he followed the assistant, he noticed Don's office door open, and a beautiful actress walked out. Her hair was messy, and she was fixing her clothes as she hurried away.

"That's weird," Johnny thought.

Once he made it to the set, Johnny looked around in amazement at the level of detail the crew had lavished on the props.

He reached into his jean pant pocket and pulled out his bottle of prescription pills discreetly. He popped a couple in his mouth before hiding the bottle back in his pocket. His fellow actors greeted Johnny as he walked up.

"Nice to meet you, Johnny. I'm Henry," one of them said, shaking Johnny's hand.

A gorgeous blonde woman ran up from behind Johnny and gave him a big hug.

"Johnny!" she said as she squeezed him tight. She was his costar for the film, Mallory Malloy. She had been voted the "Number One Up-and-Coming Actress" in *Action* magazine back in 2023.

"Nice to see you, Mallory," said Johnny. "You ready to do this or what?"

"You're damned right! It's my honor to work with you on your first starring role!" Mallory exclaimed.

"The honor is all mine," said Johnny. "Let's make some movie magic."

The rest of the cast assembled on the set, as did the directors, producers, and videographers. Billy, the set coordinator, announced that they would begin shooting in five minutes.

The actors all were dressed in their character's attire. Johnny was playing "Bruce," the lead role in *Loose Ends*. The movie was written by Julian Phillips, known for award-winning films such *Castle Run* and *Hawk Island*, who had not had a big hit in the theaters in over seven years since *Castle Run 3* bombed the opening weekend. Julian was hoping that this movie, which he wrote and was directing, would give his career newfound life and put him back into the Hollywood spotlight. Johnny was hired as a sort of experimental casting that they thought could pay off big time, especially with his new fame and virality on the internet. Julian wrote *Loose Ends* as a trilogy, and if all went well, Johnny would be brought back for the following two sequels.

While on set, Johnny tried to make himself comfortable. But it was all so surreal. He was not used to this side of things. Yet his past and history with stunt work gave him the exact background for the character he would be playing.

The lead videographer, Chris, got in his chair that then was elevated high in the air. He got in position before he shouted, "Good to go!"

"Actors, take your positions!" Tommy, the assistant director, called out.

Johnny and Mallory walked to their marked spots on the set where they would begin shooting the first scene of *Loose Ends*. Johnny straightened up his leather jacket and stretched his arms out in both directions to prepare himself.

Julian stood up from his director's chair and held his megaphone to his mouth.

A production assistant with the set clapper stood in front of the main camera. "*Loose Ends*, Scene One, Take One…."

Johnny then stretched his arms behind his back until his shoulders both cracked at the same time. Then, he cleared his throat.

The set lights grew bright as the cut-out street corner began to glow.

"Action!" Julian shouted.

Chapter Thirteen

A red light glowed on the main high-definition camera pointed at the film set. Recording had begun. Johnny took a deep breath. He looked to his left and noticed all of the cameramen pointing their devices toward him. He felt the pressure weighing on him. He knew he had to do well. Johnny's costar, Mallory, waited for Johnny to begin speaking so she could say her lines. The entire production staff watched as Johnny gazed into the bright film lights.

"Uhh," one of the producers said. "Is he ever gonna speak?"

"Not sure," another producer whispered.

Then, after about thirty seconds of silence, Johnny said his first line.

"I thought I would never get the chance to see you again."

Mallory looked away, then back at Johnny before replying, *"That is because you left when shit got too real. I never thought I'd see you again either."*

"I've thought about you every single day since then," Johnny said with a level of sincerity the entire production team could feel. The atmosphere of the set got really tense.

"Well, I've thought about you here and there myself," Mallory said with a look in her eye.

"I wanted to make things right between us," Johnny said as he inched closer to Mallory. She gravitated toward him before backing away.

"I don't think you're going to be able to do that, Bruce," she said sternly.

"Let me try, at least, Julie," Johnny said in a soft voice.

"It's not gonna be that easy!" Mallory exclaimed.

"I know. I understand. You're still mad at me for everything that went down in the past. But you have no clue what was going on with me at the time. I had to leave. It was for you and your kids' safety. I hope you know that," said Johnny.

"Yeah, fine, if that's the lie you want to tell yourself to make yourself feel better about the situation, go for it. But whatever you were dealing with, you could have told me. We could have figured it out together."

"No. We couldn't. You don't get it. It was the only way I could protect you. I had to get away. Far away. To make sure nothing ever happened to you, George, or Myra. I'm risking everything right now just to see you again," Johnny explained.

"Don't come back years later acting like you left to protect me. Or to protect us even. That's a...."

Mallory went blank for a moment.

"I'm sorry, what's the line after that?"

One of the producers read from the film script, *"That's a load of bullshit."*

"Right, okay. Sorry, I knew that. Let's start back from there," Mallory said as she fixed her posture.

"And action!" Julian shouted through his megaphone.

"That's a load of bullshit!" Mallory exclaimed dramatically.

The camera crew maneuvered their hardware around on swivels to capture different angles and shots of the scene as the two stars continued to converse.

"It's not. I was protecting you. At all costs. I don't even know why I'm here. I'm putting both of our lives at risk just speaking to you right now."

"Sure. Right. I don't even know if I believe you, you truly are a tactical agent spy or whatever you say you are," Mallory said. *"Maybe you're just another fuckboy looking for an excuse to hit it and quit it! Now you just miss me and you're giving me all these excuses when the truth is you weren't man enough to be with me then, so you up and left out of nowhere!"*

Mallory turned around and put her hands over her face and wept. Johnny stepped closer to her. He tried to place his hand on her shoulder before she smacked it away. The entire crew was in awe with their performance.

"I'm sorry I haven't been able to share everything about my past, my life, or my career. But that is not my decision. I've done a lot of things that I just can't tell anybody. Not even the one I love. And it's the worst feeling in the world. I love you every single day that goes by," Johnny went on.

Just then, Johnny and Mallory looked over and saw three stuntmen in suits and black sunglasses approaching from across the street. They all had their hands in their pockets.

"Dammit, it's already not safe," said Johnny.

"What? Who the hell is that?" she asked.

"I don't think we want to wait around to find out," Johnny said before he grabbed Mallory's hand. *"We gotta get out of here!"*

The two ran down the set street. The three men in suits began powerwalking toward them. Johnny picked up speed as he pulled Mallory's hand. They ran faster and faster. The camera crew followed closely.

"I won't let anything happen to you," Johnny said. *"I promise."*

"Okay, I am going to trust you," Mallory said while running. She was losing her breath. *"Just this time. Don't make me regret it."*

"And cut!" Julian yelled. "Terrific job!"

"Wow. That got intense, huh!" Mallory said after she took a deep breath.

"Yeah, you were really, really good," Johnny said.

"I think we might actually have legitimate chemistry," she said while catching her breath.

"I have to agree with you," Johnny said.

Johnny couldn't believe the scene was over. He was sure that he would mess up at least one of his lines. But to his surprise, he landed every line perfectly fine. He came off very naturally and that is what the director was going for. He had a blast filming and could not wait until the next scene.

"Maybe I really was born for this," Johnny said to himself as one of the production assistants handed him a water bottle.

"Let's get the set ready for the next scene!" Julian said through the megaphone.

Johnny walked away from the set for a moment. He reached into his cargo shorts pocket and pulled out his prescription painkillers. He unscrewed the cap off and popped a couple of pills into his mouth.

He wasn't even in pain at the moment, it was purely out of habit at that point.

The next scene included an action sequence that Johnny had been preparing for.

As they walked to the set, Johnny got to talking to Mallory.

"Any advice for me going into the next scene?"

"Umm, like, sure. I can't believe you're asking me for advice…" Mallory said as she began to blush.

"Well, yeah, you've been in a million movies and shows, why wouldn't I?" he asked humbly. "I've barely said more than five lines in a movie until now. It was always Cole."

"That makes sense. First off. Just be yourself. They obviously picked you for a reason. So be yourself without any shame. Whatever it takes. Sometimes you really gotta make a fool out of yourself for some good film. You know what I'm saying?" Mallory said.

"I think I do," Johnny replied.

The two of them reached the other side of the set where the crew finished putting everything in place. Johnny looked to his left and noticed something odd. It was a man with his same hair, body type, and similar face, wearing the same attire as Johnny. A leather jacket, jeans, and ripped up white tank top.

"What the hell?" Johnny said.

"Hey, nice to meet you," said the man. "My name's Matt! I'll be your stuntman."

"Hell no! Hell to the no!" Johnny exclaimed. "Everybody knows I'm doing my own stunts!"

"Umm, right. But, like, I'm here for the big…"

Johnny cut him off, "No! Fuck no. I do all my own stunts. All of them! I appreciate it, but no. Sorry bro."

"What's going on over here?" Julian, the director, asked as he hurried closer.

"What the hell is this? A stuntman? I am the stuntman! What makes you think I need a double?" Johnny asked, clearly bothered by the whole ordeal.

"Listen, Johnny. Matt is only here for the really big jumps and explosion scenes for the most part. We know you'll do all of your own action scenes. But Matt is only gonna do the dangerous stuff. We can't risk you being in any real danger. That could stop production of the film going forward, you understand?" Julian explained.

"Dude, I'm not scared of a little bit of pyro or falls, Julian. I told you, I do all my own stunts," Johnny said.

"You used to do Cole's stunts. Now it's time you get a bit of help with your own, John," said Julian.

"Ugh. Whatever. Fine. I guess he can help out for a couple of them."

"That's the spirit!" Julian said, giving Johnny a playful tap on the shoulder with the megaphone.

Johnny turned back to Matt and shook his hand. "Nice to meet you. Don't make me look like a pussy out there!"

"I won't, brother. I won't."

That night, Johnny got home from work around 10 o'clock. He let himself in and slammed the door shut.

"Oh shit! Johnny Biggs in the building!" Trevor shouted from the living room. Johnny went into the kitchen and grabbed a bottle of ice-cold beer from the fridge. He cracked the cap off with a bottle opener and walked into the living room. He greeted Trevor on the couch with a high five and took a seat next to him.

"You got here just in time, bro," Trevor said. Trevor then proceeded to light up a big fat blunt.

"Nice. How was your day, my man?" Johnny asked.

"Not too shabby, got out of work early. Got some wins in *League of Shooters*. All in all. Not too bad. How about you? How was filming?" Trevor asked as he paused his video game and gave his roommate his undivided attention.

"It was pretty…. awesome. I must say. It went really well," Johnny said.

Trevor took a few hits of the blunt before passing it over to his best friend. Johnny took a big rip as the ember lit up bright orange. He inhaled the smoke deeply before exhaling it out into a large cloud.

"Just what I needed," Johnny said before taking another big puff of the fat blunt.

"Welcome home, my friend," Trevor said, restarting the game. He tossed the other controller to Johnny. "Come on, I need some help on this new map."

Johnny caught the controller and said, "Time to light these bozos up then!"

Trevor laughed and said, "Hell yeah!"

Johnny took one more hit of the blunt before passing it back to Trevor. Smoke billowed along the ceiling of their living room and into the hallways.

Chapter Fourteen

It was Thursday night, and Johnny was up late. He looked at his phone.

"Almost three A.M.! Damn, I need to get to sleep at some point," Johnny said to himself as he sat on the couch. He'd been watching old classic western films all night. Trevor had fallen asleep on the other couch during the second movie, *Tall Tale on the East End*. It was one of Johnny's favorite movies growing up. His father used to watch it with him all the time, along with many other western and action films. The fact that he bonded with his father through films as a child had probably connected Johnny to movies when he was older.

His dad was proud to see Johnny do the stunts, but always wanted him in more important roles. He wanted to actually see his son's face on-screen. When Johnny told his parents about the new movie that he was starring in, they could not believe it. Especially his father. He was so proud and excited for the movie to be released. Johnny invited them to the set to watch him film, but they had not been able to make it there yet. Both his parents were in their eighties. But his father promised Johnny that he would make it to the set one day.

Johnny decided to switch the HDMI input to the videogame channel, and he turned on the game console. He looked over at Trevor and said, "Hey, sleepy fuck, you wanna play some *League of Shooters*?"

Trevor responded with the sounds of loud snores.

"I guess I'll be playing solo, then," Johnny replied. He picked up the controller as the game's main menu loaded.

Johnny selected the solo rumble mode and pressed the Y button. "Initiating matchmaking," the screen read. The game loading screen came on. Johnny rubbed the blur from his eyes as the night turned to early morning. Smoke hovered around the room when Johnny lit up a roach from the joint Trevor had rolled earlier. It was so big that Trevor had passed out before the two could finish it together.

League of Shooters loaded up on the screen as Johnny leaned back in his soft, cushy couch and kicked his feet up. He lifted the white controller as the game began. Johnny's avatar fell from a jet flying over the island on the map. Johnny navigated through the air, flying toward the spot he marked on the map by Whistling Hollow, one of his favorite areas to land. There were ninety-nine other players remaining. The only way to win was to be the last player standing. Johnny's avatar, dressed in a golden superhero suit and a big black cape, came crashing down to the ground. Once he landed, he ran toward a car and picked up a common assault rifle. He also picked up a few health shields on the way to a large building. Johnny's avatar heard footsteps from across the street. He hid behind a building and waited to see if anyone would show up. A few moments later, an opponent appeared, holding a legendary pistol. "Oh snap," Johnny said to himself. "I got you, punk."

Johnny's avatar crept around the building, trying not to make a large sound. He was scoping out his opponent, figuring out the best angle of attack when—out of nowhere—Johnny slid on his knees to the left of his opponent. He pressed the trigger button on the controller and blasted the other player. He shot him five times, three in the head, before he was eliminated. *JohnnyKilledYou* *eliminated* *PorkySlammer533* came across the screen. "You are god damned right," Johnny said to himself.

He lifted the fat roach from the ashtray and sparked the lighter. The joint lit up from the opposite end as Johnny took a big puff of the California Indica. He let out a big smokey cloud. The game became clearer as the colors grew more vibrant. Johnny took another puff before exhaling a second cloud of smoke into the living room air. He walked his character to the downed enemy and collected all the loot that was left.

Johnny walked around the map, running into a few enemies along the way. He took them all out with an epic purple double barrel shotgun he found in a bush on his journey to Windy Lake, which was halfway across the other side of the map from where he landed.

There were only forty-five players remaining when Johnny found a nitro-boosted motorcycle in a garage. Johnny started the bike and got it to full speed before he ran into another opponent. This one met Johnny with a rocket launcher from the second story window of a nearby house. Johnny lost a lot of health during the second rocket shot, but he managed to hide behind a dumpster. Johnny quickly used his med kit to heal up, but he could tell that the other player was creeping up on him. He heard the footsteps getting closer. Once he was healed, he switched weapons from the shotgun to the common assault rifle. Johnny could see on his radar that the enemy was to the left of him, gaining on him. Johnny jumped out from behind the dumpster and started shooting his assault rifle.

The opponent got closer and tried to melee attack Johnny, but Johnny blocked it, switched back to the shotgun, and blasted him from a couple of feet away. *JohnnyKilledYou eliminated SharpBoogers8319* came across the screen. "Let's fucking go!" Johnny yelled, almost waking Trevor. Trevor rolled over on the other couch and began snoring louder. Johnny took another hit from the joint. As it got smaller, he put it out in the ashtray. He reached over and picked up his bottle of ice-cold beer and took a big swig.

After about thirty minutes, there were only five other players besides Johnny left in the game. He had built a fort with different materials he had gathered around the map by smashing and destroying buildings, cars, and anything he came across that could be used for building.

Finally, it was down to the last two players. Johnny was doing his best, hiding in the top of the fort that he had built for himself. He had killed ten of the ninety-nine opponents in the battle royale style game. He usually played duos with Trevor, or squads with his friends online. But it was late, and he was feeling the solos game. The last opponent tried to build a long set of stairs leading up to Johnny, but Johnny was hiding behind the wall, waiting for him. The opponent smashed his way in from the ceiling, breaking down the wall before falling into the room Johnny had built for himself.

The enemy shot at him, missing the first time, but connected with Johnny's avatar's stomach. Johnny's health was low, but he threw a grenade and ran at full speed before jumping out the window and latching on to a rope that swung him away from the building just before his fort blew up. *JohnnyKilledYou eliminated JoseLopez420* came across the screen.

"That's right, bitch!" Johnny yelled at the screen as the big Victory symbol flashed. Johnny's avatar did his signature dance where he spun around before doing a backflip. "Hell yeah!" he exclaimed. "I forgot how fun this game is."

Johnny woke up around 1:30 the next afternoon. He won five times out of nine games of *League of Shooters*. That was pretty impressive considering he never really had time to play the game, unlike his roommate Trevor.

He figured he would take it easy that afternoon since he was a bit hungover. He had had a few too many beers, and one too many joints for the common man. "Damn, my head is killing me," he said as he reached into his pocket. Johnny pulled out his prescription bottle of pain killers. He popped one in his mouth, before mustering up the strength to stand and walk to the bathroom.

Trevor was in the kitchen making himself a bologna and cheese sandwich on white bread. Johnny walked out of the bathroom and into the kitchen.

"You stayed up pretty late last night, huh?" Trevor asked.

"I guess so," Johnny said. "I feel like shit."

"You look like shit, too," Trevor responded before laughing.

"Bro, I wreaked havoc in *League of Shooters* last night," Johnny said as he went into the fridge and pulled out some orange juice. He opened it and drank straight from the carton.

"Come on, man!" Trevor exclaimed.

"Chill, there's barely any left," Johnny said before finishing up the juice.

"Don't you have a date with that chick Gloria tonight?" Trevor asked.

"Oh snap, you're right," said Johnny. "I do."

"Lucky guy, huh. Better get rid of that hangover by then. You want a bologna sandwich?"

"Nah, I'm straight. Thanks, though," Johnny said.

"Suit yourself," Trevor said before he took a big bite into his sandwich.

Later that night, Johnny drove his Pompa SUV down the highway with Gloria in the passenger seat. Johnny was showing off the interior of the vehicle.

"That's really nice," Gloria said.

"Yeah, I'm not used to nice cars," Johnny said.

"Well get used to it, superstar," she said. "So, where are you taking me?"

"That's a surprise," Johnny said. "Let's just say, we're going on an adventure."

"All right, sounds fun," she said. Gloria looked out the window as Johnny turned up the volume knob. Classic rock played through the speakers. It was one of Johnny's favorite musicians, Ed Scully. His father used to play his records for him all of the time growing up. The song playing was called, "Raised by the Night." Johnny knew all the words.

"I like that you listen to this type of stuff," said Gloria. "You're different."

"Yeah, I really just despise most of the crap on the radio these days," Johnny said.

"I don't blame you," Gloria said.

The two pulled up to the valet parking attendant at a restaurant called Augustino's.

"Wow, I've heard of this place. Super fancy," she said. Johnny took her hand and helped her out of the SUV. Gloria was dressed in a beautiful black dress that shone at every angle.

"I've never been here. Figured it sounded nice," he said as he escorted her to the front entrance. When they approached the hostess, Johnny said, "Table for Mister Biggs."

The hostess looked at her guest list and said, "Right this way, Mister Biggs."

She walked them through the restaurant and to their table for two. Johnny pulled one of the seats back for Gloria to sit. She took a seat as he pushed it in for her. The hostess placed two menus on the table.

"Why, didn't know men still did that," Gloria said.

Johnny smiled and then took a seat on the other side of the table.

"Your waiter will be right with you," said the hostess.

"Thank you," said Johnny.

One of the servers placed two ice-cold glasses of water on the table and offered them some wine. "Merlot?"

"Sure, why not?" said Johnny.

The server poured two glasses of wine and walked away.

"Why thank you," said Gloria.

"Cheers," Johnny said as he lifted up his glass of Merlot.

"Cheers, to what?" Gloria asked.

"Cheers...to our careers, and our futures in showbiz!" Johnny exclaimed.

"Cheers!" Gloria said while blushing. They touched glasses and both took a sip.

"Damn, that's some good shit," said Johnny.

"Not bad at all," said Gloria.

They glanced over the menu. Johnny realized that every entrée on the menu was over thirty dollars. At first, he gulped. Then he remembered the bonus check that he got for his new movie and decided not to sweat it. "Get whatever you want, sweetie," he said.

"Somebody's balling these days, huh?" she said as she looked at the menu.

"Well, I guess I'm doing well for myself, sure."

"Honey, you're doing better than well," Gloria said.

The waiter appeared and said, "Good evening! My name is Ernesto. I will be your waiter for the evening. Might I recommend the filet mignon for Mister Biggs. And maybe the grilled Tilapia for the lady."

"Thank you, Ernesto. For now, can we just get some bread for the table," said Johnny.

"Of course, sir," said the waiter.

"Actually, I'm really starved. Is it okay if I order?" Gloria said.

"Umm, yeah, of course. My bad, I didn't realize you were so hungry."

"I haven't eaten all day," she said.

"What can I get you?" asked Ernesto.

"I would like the lobster tail and shrimp scampi with a side of loaded mashed potatoes, a blue cheese wedge salad, and some green beans, please," Gloria said.

"Damn, girl, you came ready to eat, huh?" Johnny said. "I love a girl that can eat."

"Oh, I can eat. And I told you, I'm hungry, boy," Gloria replied.

"And for you, sir?" asked the waiter.

"Umm, yeah, I'll do the filet mignon and a baked potato," Johnny said.

"How would you like your steak?"

"Rare, please," Johnny said.

"Of course, I'll have all of that out to you right away. And I will get you some bread, pronto," said Ernesto before walking away.

Johnny and Gloria first sat across from each other, but Johnny decided to move his seat next to hers so they could be closer together. Gloria found that to be extremely romantic.

The two talked the whole time as they waited for their food. Johnny asked Gloria about her life, her childhood, her family, what it was like growing up. He learned that she had three brothers and grew up in Mexico. She moved to California when she was eighteen to try to become an actress. She then fell into doing makeup work as the acting dream did not happen overnight and became more of a pipedream over time. Johnny felt for her. In his head, he was wondering how he was going to get her a part in his next movie. She was so beautiful. He knew he could make it happen. He had a feeling that she would be a great actress.

Their food finally arrived. Gloria's lobster was steaming when it got to their table. "Damn, that looks delicious," Johnny said.

"I know, right?" Gloria responded.

Johnny thought his steak smelled like the best he'd ever had. Gloria took out her phone. "Sorry, but I

114

have to," she said as she snapped some shots of the lobster and shrimp scampi.

"It looks so good," Johnny said. "I don't blame you at all. Take all the pictures you like," he said as he smiled, watching her. He thought she was so cute even though it usually made him cringe when people took photos of their food. He did not mind with her.

Once she was done with the pictures, they both began to eat. Every bite seemed to melt in their mouths. The food was breathtaking. Johnny had never had steak that good before. Gloria was using the tools they gave her for the lobster to break it open. She dipped the lobster meat into warm butter before taking a bite.

"Oh my gosh, you have to try this!" she said. "So good!"

She reached over and put a piece of buttered lobster meat into Johnny's mouth.

"Damn, you're right. Amazing."

"You know, Johnny, I was thinking about something," Gloria said.

"Oh yeah? What's that, gorgeous?"

"Well, I was thinking that once your movie came out, maybe you really could get me a role in the next one, like you said?"

Johnny stopped eating his steak for a second and put down his fork and knife.

"You know, I was already planning on talking to the producers for you. Legit," Johnny said.

"Really?" Gloria said as she sat up out of her seat and hugged him. "That would be so amazing!"

"Can you act?" Johnny asked.

"Can I act? Well of course I can! I just like to keep it real with you, darling," she said before planting a big kiss on his cheek.

"Shit, I'm sure you can. You definitely got the look to be the lead role if you ask me," Johnny said.

"Aww, you're the sweetest," said Gloria.

After dinner was over, Johnny took Gloria for a walk down the streets of downtown Los Angeles. He held her hand. They both felt very heavy after the meal. Gloria ate almost everything, even with her tiny physique. She saved a little bit of shrimp scampi for later that she took to-go.

They walked several blocks to a hole-in-the-wall nightclub called Hollywhoa. There was a line of a couple dozen people waiting to get in. Johnny walked up to the front and showed his ID. The bouncer checked the VIP list on his clipboard and said, "What's up, Johnny? Come on in!"

Johnny shook his hand and walked through the front door with Gloria on his arm. Loud house music blared through the front door. When they got inside, they could feel the bass booming. Johnny walked Gloria through the crowded dance floor of guys and girls dancing having a good time.

He walked up to the bar and ordered two Long Island iced teas. Gloria took Johnny's hand and dragged him onto the dance floor. A remix of one of her favorite songs began to play. Gloria danced as she took one of the drinks from his hands and sipped from the straw.

"That's pretty strong!" she yelled. Johnny could barely hear her.

"Take this one then! Maybe it's not so strong!" he replied.

"No, it's fine! I want it strong!"

The two danced together for a while. When another one of Gloria's favorite songs came on, she decided to pull Johnny in close. She looked at him straight in the eyes before she gave him a big kiss. The music played in the background as the two made out in the middle of the dance floor.

Johnny swayed with her back and forth as a slow song came on. He finished his drink. That's when he looked over and noticed a familiar man by the bar, staring at him. Johnny looked closer and realized that it was one of the men from the bar fight he had gotten into, standing with the same group of men. "Fuck," he said to himself. That's when the guy realized that it was Johnny and told some of his associates. They all looked at Johnny and Gloria and walked straight toward them.

"Quick, we have to go," Johnny said.

He took Gloria's hand and pulled her through the crowded dance floor, with the men in pursuit. Johnny weaved in and out of the crowd until he found a side exit. Johnny yanked the exit door open and dragged Gloria outside with him.

"What's happening?" Gloria asked as she followed Johnny down the street and away from the club.

"Long story. I'll explain later," he said as he continued down the block. Just then, one of the goons from the club jumped out from a dark alley. Johnny caught a glimpse of him at the last second, and when the guy lunged for him, Johnny did a quick spin kick to the man's jaw. This knocked him down to the ground hard. The man tried to get back up and charged at Johnny. Johnny pushed Gloria away from the man who almost got too close to her. He headbutted the man in the nose, and then tripped him with his leg making him fall into a pile of trash on the side of the road.

"Let's go!" Johnny shouted as he grabbed Gloria's hand and the two ran down the alley.

Johnny snuck her down a back road toward Augustino's. When they reached the front of the restaurant, Johnny gave the valet attendant his ticket. They brought his Pompa to the front, where Johnny and Gloria got into the car. Johnny tipped the attendant ten dollars before he sped off.

"Buckle up!" he said.

"What the hell happened back there?" Gloria asked.

"Some guys are looking for Cole. I guess he still owes them money. For some reason, they think I'm him," Johnny explained as he swerved right onto the street and sped through a red light.

"That's crazy that they think he's you, I mean, you two sort of look alike I suppose," Gloria said as she looked in the rear-view mirror to see if anyone was following them. Johnny sped down the road even faster.

"I told you tonight would be an adventure," Johnny said while breathing heavily.

"You weren't lying," she replied.

"Let's get back to my place, watch a movie or something," Johnny said as he continued driving down the road at sixty miles per hour in a thirty-five MPH zone.

"That sounds like a great idea," said Gloria. "Just drive safe, handsome. And please slow down."

Johnny nodded and said, "Yes, ma'am," just before swerving right onto Jefferson Avenue.

Chapter Fifteen

Johnny was called by Don Steiner's assistant to meet with Don on Monday. Johnny showed up to the producer's office in a slick pinstriped blue suit with a white button down underneath, and a silver tie going down his chest. He was wearing slacks and fancy shiny black dress shoes. He topped off the outfit with a brand-new golden diamond-crusted watch and $200 Da Vinci sunglasses. He signed in with the receptionist, Priscilla, at the front desk.

While he waited, Johnny wondered what Don wanted to see him about. He reached into his pocket for his prescription pills and casually popped one into his mouth. He was nervous, but he was not sure why.

A couple of minutes later, Priscilla said, "Johnny Biggs, Don will see you now."

Johnny got up from his seat and walked down the hallway until he reached a door that read *Don Steiner*. Johnny knocked on the door, which was already cracked open.

"Come on in," said Don. Johnny pushed the door open wide and stepped into the lavish office of one of Hollywood's topmost prestigious producers.

"Don, how the hell are ya?" Johnny asked as he shook the beefy film mogul's hand.

"Never been better," Don said. "Take a seat, sit down."

Johnny settled into the seat in front of the large marble desk in the middle of Don's humungous office.

"Julian showed me an early screening of some scenes from *Loose Ends*. I'm loving what I'm seeing. And boy, you're really knocking it out of the park," Don said.

He stood and walked to the bar by the side of the office. He lifted a bottle of bourbon and unscrewed the top. He took two glasses and opened his ice box. He took the scooper and scooped three ice cubes into each glass. Then, Don poured the age-old bourbon into the glasses until they were about halfway full.

"Here, have a drink with an old timer," said Don.

"Don't mind if I do," said Johnny as he took the glass. They clinked their cups together and both took a drink. Johnny made a face like it tasted good yet strong.

"That's ten years old right there," said Don. "The older the better, I tell you."

"Not bad at all," said Johnny as he took another sip. He could feel the hairs on his chest stand up with every drop going down his gullet.

"I'm glad you're here, John. I wanted to talk to you about another motion picture you'd be perfect for," said Don.

"Oh yeah? Already another one?" asked Johnny as he made himself comfortable in his chair.

"Well, I thought you could be great in this new horror movie. I just read the script; it's called *Hang Nail*. I don't know why, but when I read the script, I could see you playing the main character, 'Harrison.' I just saw your face when I was reading it. I figured I had to see if you were interested," Don went on. He took another swig of the bourbon. "Ah, good stuff."

"I'd love to. Whatever you want, boss. I'm your man. I'm trying to expand my horizons," said Johnny as he took a drink.

"Well, first, let me send you the script and make sure it is something that you'd like to do, but I think you'll agree that you would be a perfect fit."

"Sounds great. Send it to my agent, Cashew Peters."

"Already sent it to him," Don said before winking.

Johnny thought for a second and said, "You know? I have a great actress that could be in it too, if there is a good role for a female, of course. I just guessed since it's a horror movie, then there's gotta be a main female character."

"Oh yeah? Who is that?" asked Don.

"My friend, Gloria Jimenez. She's a very talented, beautiful, upcoming actress. She's actually my makeup artist on *Loose Ends*. But I truly believe she has what it takes," said Johnny.

"Hmm, I guess I can give your girlfriend a shot. I'm guessing she is your girlfriend, right?" Don turned to the right, then looked back at Johnny with a slightly creepy grin on his face.

"Well, yeah, something like that. But it would really mean a lot to me," he said.

"Tell her to come in for an interview. I'll see what I can do, buddy," Don said.

"I really appreciate it, boss," said Johnny as he finished the rest of the bourbon.

"Listen, you read that *Hang Nail* script and get back to me by the end of the week."

"Will do," said Johnny.

"And I'll have Cashew set something up with this Gloria you speak of," said Don.

"That would be great," Johnny said. "I owe you one."

"Don't mention it."

Johnny got up and shook Don's hand, "Guess I gotta run. We gotta film one of the last scenes for *Loose Ends* in a couple of hours. It involves this huge stunt I'm really excited about doing."

"But you know you're not actually doing that jump, right? With the explosion?" Don said.

"That's the one," Johnny said. "But what do you mean? They said I could do some of my own stunts."

"Not that one. We're gonna need your double to do that one for you. I can't have my future megastar getting hurt just because he wants to show off his big balls, you got me?" said Don.

Johnny turned away to roll his eyes, then turned back and said, "Yeah, I guess that makes sense. You're the boss, whatever you say."

"Trust me," said Don. "I only have your best interests in mind, John."

"I believe you," he said.

Johnny walked toward the door and said, "Talk to you soon, Don. Thanks again for everything."

"Don't mention it," Don said as he poured himself another glass of bourbon.

As Johnny was leaving the office, a folder on a shelf by the door caught his eye. He noticed an emblem. It was a hexagon-shaped logo that looked very similar to the one on the van that tried to kidnap the little girl he'd saved months before.

That's odd, Johnny thought as he walked out the door.

The next week flew by as Johnny and the rest of the crew wrapped up filming *Loose Ends*. They traveled to a few locations in rural California to film different b-roll and action chase scenes. Since most of the filming was done on set in Hollywood, Johnny enjoyed the chance to travel a bit for the movie. But everywhere he went, he felt like he had eyes on him from Don Steiner.

It was the last day of filming. Mallory was on set talking to Johnny about her niece's ballet recital that she'd attended the night before. Johnny was trying not to fall asleep. Not only because he was uninterested in the story, but because he had gotten less than three hours of sleep the night before. He had been spending a lot of time with Gloria lately as they were getting closer and closer.

"And then, my little sweet niece, Paula, did like five spins in a row before doing a split, I couldn't believe it. I was so proud of her," Mallory said.

"That's so cool," Johnny said, barely taking in what his co-star was telling him.

"Are you even listening?" Mallory asked.

"To be honest...barely," Johnny responded.

"Ugh, you're lame," said Mallory as she turned away from Johnny and started talking to their other co-star, Richard.

"Thank god," Johnny said to himself as he took a seat on a bench to wait for their final scene to begin filming. He tried to rest his eyes for a few moments.

Just then, he got a text from Gloria that read, "Hey Baby!"

Johnny texted back, "Hey hun, how are you?"

"I can't believe you came through!" her next text read. "Your agent Cashew called me to set up a meeting with Don Steiner!"

Johnny smiled and wrote, "I'm glad to help." He sent a smiling emoji followed by a heart.

"You're the best, babe," Gloria texted. "Have a great day on set!"

"Thanks babe," Johnny wrote back.

"All right, actors, places! Final scene begins in five minutes!" one of the producers on set announced.

Johnny and the crew filmed the last scene that included a very emotional performance by Johnny and his co-star Mallory, who stole the performance with her ability to act serious, yet funny at times.

The two had a lot of chemistry together by the end of filming *Loose Ends*. Directors and writers were already at work on the sequel before they even finished shooting the first. There was talk of it becoming a trilogy franchise. It all depended on how successful the first one would become with a virtually unknown actor, Johnny Biggs, in the lead role.

The last scene came to a close when Julian got on the megaphone to shout, "And that's a wrap! Thank you all for everything you have contributed to this film! We could not do it without each and every one of you!"

The director then began clapping for all of his actors and crew on the set.

Mallory hugged Johnny. Johnny shook the hands of everyone on the crew, from the cameramen to the stuntmen, to the production assistants, and everyone in between. He was very humble and took time to pose for pictures with anyone who asked and talked with everyone on set. He felt no bigger or more important than anyone else. He hung out with the stuntmen and told them stories of his years doing stunt work for Cole Tillman.

Johnny was kind of sad that it was all over. It was bittersweet because he was also excited to see how the movie turned out. He couldn't wait until opening night. He knew he still had voiceovers he had to record, but most of his work was done. He got in his Pompa SUV and drove out of the set parking lot and headed back home.

The next day, Gloria had a one o'clock appointment with Don Steiner. She called Johnny before to make sure they were still on for dinner that night.

Gloria waited in Don's waiting room until Priscilla called her name.

"Gloria? Don will see you now," his receptionist said.

Gloria stood up in her stunning red dress, red lipstick, and leather jacket. She was dressed to impress the producer.

Priscilla walked Gloria through the hallway until they reached Don's office. Priscilla knocked on the door and said, "Mister Steiner, your one o'clock is here."

"Come in," Don said.

Priscilla looked at Gloria and said, "Good luck, cutie."

Gloria walked inside the magnificent office.

"Thank you, Priscilla," Don said. "Shut the door, please and thank you." He turned to Gloria. "Come in, take a seat."

Before sitting down, she gave him a kind of awkward hug and a weak kiss on the cheek, to which he tried to turn his head to catch more of her lips. But he missed.

Gloria took a seat in the chair and scooted back a bit away from the desk. Don went around to his side of the table and sat down in a chair that might as well have been a throne.

"Thank you for meeting with me," Gloria said. "I appreciate you taking the time out of your day."

"It's my pleasure," said Don. "Johnny has told me wonderful things about you."

"Oh, Johnny's the best," she said while blushing.

"He is. He really is," said Don.

"So, like, do you want me to audition, or...?" she asked.

"Well, I was telling Johnny about this upcoming horror movie we want him in. And perhaps there may be a role for you. The question you have to ask yourself is, how bad do you want it?" Don said.

"Very bad, Mister Steiner," said Gloria.

Don stood up and crept to the other side of his desk.

"What would you like me to do?" she asked.

"That's a good question," Don said, "What are you comfortable doing?"

He then walked behind her and put his hands on her shoulders and began massaging them. A couple of seconds later she jumped and squirmed her way out of the chair and away from the producer.

"Not that, I'm not comfortable with that," she said.

"Oh, come on, do you know how many actresses, better yet, stars, have come into this office and left with a smile on their faces?"

"I'm sure there have been a lot," Gloria said with a petrified look in her eye.

"So, what makes you any better than them? They all had to do it," Don said.

"Well. I won't," she said.

"Well then. Why should I put you in a movie?" Don asked.

"Because I am a great actress!" Gloria exclaimed.

"I mean, you're acting like you don't want me, but that's all I see," he said.

"Well, I don't. And I won't give my body and sell my soul like that!"

"Not sure if I see you in any of my movies then."

Gloria turned to leave. Then she turned back around and said, "Is there anything I can do for a role that does not involve me having to do anything I'm not comfortable with?"

"Hmm. Show me your tits," the producer said in a creepy tone.

"What?" she asked,

"Show me your tits and I'll help you out," he said.

"If I show you my boobs for five seconds, you will give me a shot?"

"I guess we'll have to see how good they are."

Trying to muster up her last bit of dignity, Gloria tugged her dress down, revealing her breasts to the producer. He watched in awe for a few moments before she pulled it back up.

Before he could say anything, Gloria cut him off and said, "Now, do I get a speaking part in the movie with Johnny? Or do I have to sue you for sexual harassment?"

Don rolled his eyes, looked left, then looked back at her and said, "Fine, you can be in the movie. You won't be the star, but I'll make sure they find something for you."

"Why thank you, sir. That is too kind," she said. She held back tears, a bit disoriented from the experience. She could not believe she could expose herself like that. However, it was her dream to be in movies.

"Don't mention it," said Don as he opened his bourbon and drank it straight from the bottle.

"It was nice meeting with you today, Mister Steiner. Thank you for the opportunity, I will not let you down," Gloria said. She opened his office door, walked out, and slammed the door shut behind her.

Chapter Sixteen

A couple of months went by, and post-production on *Loose Ends* was wrapping up. Johnny was called in to reshoot some scenes with Mallory. He also spent about a week doing voiceover work. Julian always made sure to re-record all of the dialogue shot between the actors throughout the film.

Johnny and Gloria were becoming more intimate. About two months into dating, Johnny asked her to move in with him and his roommate Trevor. Gloria agreed and soon she moved all of her personal belongings into their townhouse.

Within a week of moving in, she convinced Johnny to get a new king-sized bed. It was much bigger than the beat-up queen-sized bed that he had had for so many years before that. She also had him redesign much of the interior of his townhouse. She had an eye for design and really spruced up the place.

One of the biggest changes was the color of the wallpaper. It went from boring old grey to a calming light blue color. Truth be told, Johnny was really happy with all of the changes. Gloria also made the house a lot cleaner overall. She had Johnny and Trevor doing more chores, and the difference was night and day. It was clear that a woman had moved in. And

Johnny could not be happier. He felt like he was actually in love. Like he may have found "the one."

That Friday, Johnny and Gloria got dressed up for the first red carpet premiere of *Loose Ends* in downtown Los Angeles for the LA Film Festival.

Johnny wore an all-white suit with a black tie and white pants. He matched it with all-black dress shoes with white laces. Gloria looked quite dazzling in a lime green sparkling dress with bright white high heels. Johnny bought her a beautiful diamond necklace to wear to the premiere. She had never been given anything that lavish before. She almost didn't feel right wearing it, that it was way too fancy for her. Johnny disagreed. He thought it was made just for her.

Instead of taking his Pompa SUV this time, the studio sent a stretch limousine to pick up Johnny and his guests. He was able to add Trevor to his VIP list, so he tagged along with them as well.

By the time the limo showed up outside their home, Johnny was just finishing getting ready. Gloria smelled beautiful from the perfume Johnny got her the week before. Trevor walked out of his room in a sky-blue button-down shirt and black pants. He got his hair cut short, and he was clean shaven for the premiere.

The three of them walked toward the limousine. Trevor opened the back door and hopped in. Johnny took Gloria's hand and helped her inside the door and followed behind. The three sat in the back of the limo. Trevor immediately went to check out the bar and what drinks they had. He took a bottle of expensive tequila and cracked open the lid. Trevor poured himself a little cup and said, "Don't mind if I do."

"I'll take some," said Gloria as she sat back in her seat. Johnny closed the door, and the limo drove away down the block.

"This is so sick. I have never even been in one of these," said Trevor.

"Get used to it," Johnny said. "This is only the beginning," he said with confidence.

Gloria cuddled up to him just when Johnny's phone began to vibrate. It was Cole calling. Johnny had not spoken to Cole in over a month. Word around town was that Cole was missing. Others said he was overseas in Japan shooting a new film. Johnny waited a moment before he clicked the answer button on the screen.

"Cole, what's going on? Where you been?"

"Johnny! My man! I just wrapped up something we were shooting in Tokyo. You should have been there!" Cole exclaimed through the phone speaker.

"I probably should have," Johnny said as he looked around at the incredible decor of the inside of the limousine. He was in awe.

"Listen, I know it sounds bad. But your pal got himself into some hot water with some powerful guys last year. Got into a debt I couldn't really get out of."

"But Cole, you have money. How do you owe these guys so much?" Johnny asked.

"It's not that simple. As I tried to explain to you before, I don't really have any liquid cash. It's all tied up in investments, the houses, cars, and on top of that…I'm addicted to gambling if you can't tell. I bet it all on this college basketball game last year…and I lost," Cole went on.

"You don't have to explain yourself to me," Johnny said. "You've done enough for me, Cole. I don't give a damn who comes looking for you, I got

131

your back. And if it's money you need, just say the word."

"You are one real motherfucker," Cole's voice echoed through the speaker of the phone. "But I can't ask my stunt double for money."

"I'm more than that these days, bro. But hey, listen, Cole. I'm gonna have to give you a call tomorrow. I'm on the way to the *Loose Ends* premiere at the LA Film Festival."

"Oh nice! I remember when my movies still debuted at those festivals!" Cole said. "Sounds good, John. I'll give you a call tomorrow. And listen, you won't have to worry about those guys running up on you anymore, I am going to take care of my debt and pay it off. Very soon."

"I believe you, Cole. And I believe in you," said Johnny.

"Same brother. Johnny, I'm proud of you," said Cole.

Johnny looked over at Gloria and Trevor who both had smiles from cheek to cheek. "Thanks Cole, talk soon." Johnny hung up the phone and put his arm around Gloria. The stretch limousine made a left onto Jefferson Street.

Fifteen minutes later, the long car pulled up in front of the red carpet of the festival. There were photographers taking pictures of Mallory up ahead. The door of the limousine swung open. First, Trevor came through the door. Then, Gloria stepped outside looking fabulous. Johnny followed behind and shut the limo door.

The photographers turned their attention toward Johnny and began snapping photos.

"There he is! Mister Biggs! Johnny Biggs!" Mallory shouted as she walked over and gave her costar a hug and a kiss on the cheek. She greeted Gloria as they knew each other from makeup and wardrobe.

Once inside, Johnny was seated by an usher toward the middle of some of the best seats in the house. The entire auditorium was full of people as the premiere was sold out. This festival only showed the best of the finest films that were due out the next year or two. *Loose Ends* was one of the most anticipated movies to be shown all weekend. Gloria and Trevor sat on both sides of Johnny.

A couple of minutes later, the opening credits began. The lights went dark, and the volume got louder through the speakers. Johnny heard his own voice come on: *"That was the night I would never forget,"* he said as the crowd began to clap. Johnny looked around and noticed the crowd seemed to be into it. The movie had begun.

Johnny spent the next two hours overthinking every gesture and reaction he could catch from the surrounding audience of *Loose Ends*. For the most part, people seemed to laugh and cheer during the right moments. But Johnny was not sure if that would be a typical crowd reaction, or if he was just lucky this time. He was not sure what to believe. But the overall reaction from the first showing definitely came off very positive.

When the end credits rolled, the crowd erupted in a standing ovation. Johnny could not believe his eyes. The movie was actually a hit in that theater at that moment. Gloria squeezed Johnny's hand tightly. She then planted a big juicy kiss on his cheek. The crowd applauded for a long while as the final song played and the names of the actors and actresses scrolled down the black screen for the closing credits.

Starring…

"Johnny Biggs" was the first name to appear.

Johnny watched his name scroll down the screen with the utmost pride. He'd finally made it in his eyes.

"That was sooo lit," Trevor said. He patted his best friend on the back. "Great job, bruh. Fire!"

"I appreciate it, yo," Johnny replied. They slapped each other's hands.

"Amazing job, babe," Gloria added.

"Thank you."

Surrounding festivalgoers walked up to Johnny to shake his hand. Many gave him credit for his acting, while others fanned out over the stunts and action sequences. One thing was for sure, Johnny had a hit on the way.

Johnny, his roommate, and his girlfriend all left the theater and walked out into the lobby where more fans bombarded Johnny. Many asked him for selfies with their phones, and Johnny obliged happily. He posed with dozens of people for pictures, and even signed some autographs on whatever people could find. He was an instant star, and the movie was still set to premiere in theaters six months from then.

Gloria watched as her boyfriend was hyped up by the crowd. At first, she was proud to be with him. After a while, she got jealous and annoyed as it kept going. She just wanted to leave; she was getting hungry. Johnny could tell when he looked at her. "I'm sorry, but we have to go," he said as he eased away from the crowd in the cinema lobby and headed out the front door with his friends.

Johnny, Gloria, and Trevor walked onto the streets where they saw the director of the film, Julian, being interviewed by a reporter.

Johnny shook Julian's hand. "They loved it in there, huh?" the director said to Johnny.

"They sure did," Johnny replied.

Johnny, Gloria, and Trevor walked down the street, leaving the limousine to wait for them out front.

"I need to get some fresh air, maybe we can go for a walk for a little bit before we head out?" Johnny said.

"That's fine, honey," said Gloria as she followed Johnny.

Johnny reached into his pant pocket and pulled out his bottle of prescription painkillers. He unscrewed the cap and popped two into his mouth as he kept walking.

"That's enough," said Gloria as she slapped his hand away and took his bottle from him. She put the orange bottle in her purse and said, "No more."

The three continued down the street for a couple of minutes. Johnny looked over and leaned into Trevor's ear. He whispered, "Hey, pull out your phone and hit record for me."

Trevor looked at Johnny, then without hesitation pulled out his phone. He opened the lock screen and pressed record.

Johnny turned to Gloria, reached into his pocket, and pulled out a tiny box. He looked at her for a moment and said, "I've been meaning to ask you something."

"Oh yeah? What are you doing?" Gloria asked.

Then, Johnny dropped down to one knee. He looked up at Gloria and said, "Will you marry me?"

She immediately blushed bright red. Tears filled her eyes. Within moments, Gloria responded, "Yes, yes. Of course, I will."

Trevor filmed the entire moment. The two kissed as Johnny showed Gloria the engagement ring that he had bought her. She could not believe how beautiful the diamond was. He placed the ring on her finger. They kissed again. Johnny stumbled back up to his feet.

Trevor finished filming as the three of them walked back to the limousine. Gloria was starving, and Johnny had promised her some dinner. They all got inside the limo, which took them to a local steakhouse called Primo. Johnny placed his arm around Gloria as the long stretch car drove away down the street.

Chapter Seventeen

Johnny rolled over in his king-sized bed next to Gloria, who was only in a bra and panties. He picked up the phone from his nightstand. It was a quarter past two in the morning. He had woken up from a bad dream and could not go back to sleep.

Johnny opened the banking app on his phone to see that a check for $425,000 had cleared into his bank account, which showed a new balance of $635,429.38. He rubbed his eyes and looked closer at his phone screen.

"Holy shit," he said to himself.

Gloria began speaking gibberish in her sleep. Johnny put on one of his favorite TV shows, *Murder Creek* on the Babylon Prime Video network playing on his 69-inch flat screen high-definition television mounted to the wall. He made sure the volume was low so it would not wake Gloria. He plugged his phone into the charger connected to the outlet on the other wall. He placed it on the nightstand and laid back. He was up to Season Three, Episode Eight. He could not stop watching it since he had found it a week prior. He was instantly hooked. Gloria did not like the series that much, definitely not as much as Johnny so he did not feel bad watching it without her. His favorite character was Derek because he saw himself in him. He thought Derek was a total badass just like himself.

Johnny thought about all the money in his bank account and started thinking about buying another house. He figured he would research the housing market and see what he could afford for Gloria, Trevor, and himself. After about thirty minutes of watching *Murder Creek*, Johnny finally fell back into a deep slumber.

The next day, Johnny and Trevor were out and about in the four-door Pompa SUV. Trevor was driving as Johnny looked out the window at different houses for sale in Beverly Hills. Johnny figured they should start looking for a bigger place. He offered Trevor the chance to continue living with Gloria and himself there. Trevor thought he was moving a little too fast, but the money was real, so he was not going to stop Johnny even if he thought it could be a big financial mistake. Especially in the current, horrible housing market.

Johnny saw a bunch of beautiful gigantic houses he really liked, but when he looked up the prices of the homes online, many were out of his price range. They decided to take a trip toward Santa Monica. Trevor found a few nice neighborhoods that had a lot of open real estate.

"Hey, let's turn here," said Johnny. Trevor made a left onto Porcupine Drive and drove half a mile.

"Whatever you say, dawg," Trevor replied as he took a hit of his marijuana vape pen.

"There, pull in here," Johnny said. His eyes widened as they pulled up to the green home with a big yard and a white door up the front steps.

"Whoa, this is pretty damn nice," Trevor said as he put the car in park in the driveway.

"This is it. This one is amazing," Johnny said.

"Well, let's call the broker and see what they'll take for it," Trevor said. "If we take out a mortgage, I think you'll be able to watch your money better than buying it in full."

"I agree," Johnny said. "But honestly, whatever it costs. I want it. I don't even care."

"It is quite lit if you ask me," Trevor said.

"Lit as fuck," Johnny added.

They got out of the car and circled around the house. Johnny walked through an open gate on the side. Trevor followed him to the backyard. It was very spacious, at least three acres—unusual for that area.

"This is the one," Johnny said after they both looked around at the majestic greenery that surrounded them. "All right, just gotta see the inside," he said as they walked back toward the front yard. He made a note of the realtor's phone number on the "For Sale" sign. They returned to the car and drove away.

Trevor made a right onto Roselawn Street and accelerated the large vehicle to fifty miles per hour. There were not many other cars on the street. Trevor took a hit of his vape pen and passed it over to Johnny. Johnny pressed the button and inhaled. He took a really long pull and ended up nearly coughing up a lung.

Trevor continued down the road until Johnny pointed out a sedan that was flipped over on the other side of the road. It looked like it had been hit by a van that had stopped about ten feet away.

"Pull over!" Johnny exclaimed. Trevor immediately pulled the SUV over to the side of the road. Johnny got out quickly and ran toward the red sedan.

Smoke billowed from the engine. The car was completely upside-down with the roof crushed on the ground. He could not tell at first if anyone was still inside, only that the airbag had been deployed.

Johnny looked more closely and saw an elderly woman strapped in the front driver seat. She must have been in her late eighties or so. "Oh shit!" Johnny exclaimed.

Trevor ran over to the second vehicle to make sure the older gentleman driving the van was okay. He seemed fine for the most part. "You okay, sir?" Trevor asked the man.

"I'll be okay. How is the other person?" the man asked.

"We're not sure, I'm going to go see how my friend is doing," Trevor replied. He hurried back toward the flipped sedan.

In the meantime, Johnny sprang into action to rescue the elderly lady. He climbed into the passenger side and reached over to unbuckle her seatbelt. She appeared to be knocked out, possibly by the force of the airbag going off. As Johnny struggled to free her, Trevor noticed the hood of the car catch fire.

"Johnny!" Trevor yelled from the other side of the car. "Time to move!"

Johnny continued to ease the frail little lady from her seat. Trevor tried to help as the fire got bigger and bigger.

"Johnny! Get the hell out of there! Here!" Trevor pulled on the lady while Johnny pushed from the other side. She was finally free. Trevor pulled her all the way out and across the road and onto the grass.

She appeared to be conscious and breathing, but she was out of it. Johnny was still trying to wriggle backwards to get himself out of the passenger side of the mangled car. By the time he managed to escape, the heat from the engine fire had gotten so hot that he knew he had to run. He made it five feet away from the car when it exploded. The force made Johnny fly in the air before crashing down to the ground hard.

"No!" Trevor yelled. He ducked behind the other car when the sedan exploded. Trevor then ran over to Johnny who was lying on the ground, burnt and bloodied. Johnny was out cold. Trevor flipped him over to his side. He did not know what to do to revive his friend. Trevor reached into his pocket, took out his smart phone, and dialed 9-1-1.

"9-1-1, what is your emergency?" a dispatcher asked from the other end of the call.

"I need paramedics to US-14 and some street I can't make out from this far away," said Trevor as he peered toward the street sign. "Chester Road."

"An ambulance is on the way. What happened?" the voice asked.

"A bad car accident. The drivers seem all right, but my friend who helped one of them is not. There was an explosion. Please send them now!" Trevor exclaimed.

He stood over Johnny, helpless, waiting for the paramedics. Johnny lay motionless on the ground with big burn marks on his forehead and gashes on his shoulders. He was hurt really badly.

By the time the ambulance arrived ten minutes later, Johnny had started to regain consciousness. But he was sore, burnt, and cut up. The paramedics came in groups, with some of them aiding the crash victims, and others aiding Johnny. They put Johnny on a stretcher and propped him up into the ambulance.

Trevor hopped back in the SUV so he could follow them to whatever hospital they would take him to.

Johnny spent one night in the hospital so the doctors could evaluate him closely and make sure more damage was not done to his body or brain.

Gloria joined Trevor in the hospital waiting room. Trevor had sent her a text on his way to the hospital. She was there thirty minutes later. She took a taxi over as soon as she heard the news.

"Where is he?" Gloria asked frantically as she came up and hugged Trevor.

"He's in room 12. They said we can't see him at the moment," he replied.

"What the hell happened?" she asked as she took a seat next to Trevor.

"Well, we were out looking for houses. I'm sure you know Johnny wants to move now that he's got money," Trevor said.

"I had no clue," Gloria responded. "You were house hunting?"

"Oh, maybe that was supposed to be a surprise," he said. "Sorry, anyway. Yeah, so, we drove by this bad accident on the side of the road. Nobody had seen it; we were the first to drive by, I guess. Johnny went to save this little old lady. And boom. It was like a fucking bomb went off," Trevor explained.

"Did Johnny save her?" Gloria asked.

"It's Johnny, what the hell do you think?"

"Right, had to be the fucking hero like always," Gloria said angrily.

"He did. He saved the shit out of her. And just like that, the car turned into a fireball. I can't believe he's not dead," Trevor said. He took his weed pen out of his pocket and took a big hit. "Want some?"

"No, thanks," Gloria said. "Any clue when we will be able to see him?"

"Not sure yet, hopefully soon," Trevor said.

"Wish you two would just stay out of trouble sometimes. It's always something with you. Johnny is going to get himself killed one of these days trying to save the world. How can he protect me when he is always trying to protect everyone else?" Gloria asked.

"All I know is, that is the man you want to be with. That's a real motherfucka right there. If he would save a woman from a burning car before it explodes, imagine what he would do for the woman that he loves?" Trevor responded.

This made Gloria stop and think for a second. A tear rolled down her face before she said, "I just don't want to lose him."

"Same," Trevor said. "And we won't. Johnny is one tough bastard."

"You're right," Gloria said as she sat back in the waiting room chair and put her head on Trevor's shoulder for support. Another tear fell. She was very eager to see Johnny. She prayed that he would be okay. Trevor prayed with her.

The two slept in the waiting room that night until the next morning when the doctor would let them see Johnny once he was stable.

Johnny barely knew where he was when Trevor and Gloria came in that morning to check on him. Gloria ran inside room 12 and gave Johnny a big kiss. He could barely kiss her back, but he did smile when he saw them. "Glad to see you two," Johnny mustered up the strength to say.

"Same, bro, same," Trevor said.

Chapter Eighteen

A month passed by, and Johnny was officially healed up and ready for his next film. In the meantime, Johnny had purchased a large, five-bedroom home for Gloria, Trevor, and himself to live in. There was a big backyard, with a fairly large pool and a brand-new hot tub a few feet away. The first green house that Johnny wanted to purchase had been sold while he was in the hospital, but thankfully he found another one that he loved. Johnny paid a big down payment for the house and got a twenty-year mortgage. Johnny gave Gloria his credit card to furnish the house however she saw fit. He just asked that he and Trevor could get to design the mancave to their desire.

Gloria repainted the walls sky blue and decked out the living room with a beautiful three panel suede couch wrapped around the walls of the room. She had a large, beautiful crystal chandelier installed in the dining room and bought a big redwood table for them to eat dinner. She bought Trevor the waterbed that he had always wanted. She got clapper lights for their bedroom. She thought they were the coolest thing in the world. Johnny did not love them as much as she did. But he did not mind. He just wanted her to be happy. He was head over heels in love with Gloria.

Trevor and Johnny would go over the scripts he was being sent to review for possible future movie roles. Johnny did not like many of them. But Gloria could see herself acting in some with him, so he read every single script with her in mind.

The more money that Johnny was making with the international success of *Loose Ends*, the more his habits began to change. Unfortunately, Gloria had a secret that she had kept from Johnny for the longest time. But finally, Gloria put both Johnny and Trevor on to one of her favorite pastimes, cocaine. She had given it up for a while, right around the time she met Johnny and throughout their courtship. But once she had moved in with Johnny and she had more money in her bank account than she knew what to do with, she went back to the addicting drug. One night, she asked Johnny and Trevor if they wanted to do it with her after a nice night out for dinner. Johnny had not done any since he was in his early twenties, but he wanted to impress Gloria so badly that he obliged. "Just this once," Johnny told her.

Trevor enjoyed cocaine from time to time, but Gloria got him to do it more and more. After a week or two, even though Johnny had originally planned to just do it once, Johnny was hooked. He was now taking his prescription pain pills as usual, but he was also ingesting a couple of grams of cocaine four to five days a week. He loved how it made him feel, and he knew Gloria loved it so much. He did not love the next day when he would come down, so he would usually just do more, so he would not crash.

One night, Johnny and Trevor stayed up all night writing a script themselves. Completely fueled by cocaine, the two wrote almost an entire script in one night. Johnny thought it was the greatest masterpiece they could have put together. Trevor agreed. However, when they both reread it soberly a couple of days later, they were not as impressed with their work.

Still…the drug gave them a level of confidence neither had experienced in a long time. Johnny felt like he was on top of the world. He had fans writing to him and sending him messages every day, every hour, praising *Loose Ends* and asking him when his next movie would be out. He had already gone viral for saving the girl from being kidnapped and getting into a wild bar fight. But now, he was making a name for himself in the movie industry. Talk shows were booking him for appearances left and right. Johnny's agent, Cashew Peters, would not stop calling him with different offers for roles in film and television. Johnny was being very particular about what he wanted to do. He wanted to create a legacy of great work. He thought most of the scripts he was being offered were cheesy and lazy. He wanted to play more serious roles with depth to the characters.

"Dude, I think this is it!" Trevor exclaimed as he threw a thick script onto the sofa.

"What's that?" Johnny asked before snorting a three-inch line of cocaine off of the coffee table with a short straw. "Whoo!" he exclaimed.

"You should do this fucking movie, dawg," Trevor said. He walked over to the coffee table and did a line of coke himself. There were four more lines left on the table. The two were on a long binge reading scripts, doing drugs, listening to loud electronic music, and playing videogames in between. They were trying to figure out the next movie that Johnny should do.

"This shit is called *Passionate Chaos*. And it is so fucking perfect for you, my G," said Trevor. "You need to read that shit, pronto."

"Oh yeah?" Johnny said as he picked up the thick packet of paper. Johnny opened it and read the first page.

"Writing seems pretty good so far, you sure this is the one?" Johnny asked as he kept reading and skimming through the first dozen pages. His pupils dilated as the white in his eyes grew red.

Trevor picked up a blunt from the ashtray and lit it up. Smoke filled the air around them.

Johnny popped a couple of prescription pain pills out of the bottle and swallowed them. Then he did another long line of cocaine. "Whoo! That's good shit." His vision blurred in and out of focus.

"When do you and Gloria start filming for *Hang Nail*?" Trevor asked.

"Two weeks from now."

"Well, read this script. They want an answer by Friday. We can have Cashew hook the meeting up. I bet you can get at least seven figures for this one," Trevor said.

"You really think so?" Johnny pondered.

"I know so, bro. You're the fucking shit. You're the next big thing, come on now!"

"Fuck it, you're right. I am the fucking shit."

"Let's get this bread," Trevor said.

"Let's get it," Johnny agreed.

Johnny threw on his fancy diamond crusted black shades. He then picked up his new brown leather jacket that Gloria had recently gifted him. He stretched for a second before leaving the room with the script in hand. "I'm going to read this and let you know. But I trust you, Trev."

"Shit, I know you do. Why wouldn't you?" he responded before laughing.

Johnny went into his large empty bedroom and tossed the leather jacket onto his king-sized bed. Then, he dropped down to do some pushups. After a set of forty, he flipped over to his back. After thirty seconds of lying there, he did some sit-ups. After about fifty, he stopped. On the ground, breathing heavily, Johnny opened up his phone. He turned it off of Airplane Mode for a second, to see his phone flooded with notifications, mostly comments and messages from friends and family ranting and raving about his blockbuster hit, *Loose Ends*. His Aunt Jody told him she's "gone out to see it three times in theaters already."

His MyFace profile had hundreds of new friend requests. He didn't feel like reading and responding to so many people, so he decided to put his phone back on Airplane Mode and continue about his day. He got up off the floor and walked out of his bedroom and down the long hallways of his new mini mansion in the suburbs of Los Angeles. He got to the living room and opened the glass doors to the backyard.

As he approached the pool area, he heard a voice say, "Is that my handsome future husband?"

"You know it," Johnny responded as he walked over to Gloria who was floating on an inflatable bed. She was in a bright red two-piece swimsuit. Johnny could not take his bloodshot eyes off of her.

"Come on in," Gloria said as she sipped her blueberry margarita through a straw.

"Don't mind if I do," he said before doing a big cannonball into the pool splashing water everywhere.

Johnny swam up to the surface of the water and floated over to Gloria. He gave her a kiss and swam away. As he came up from the water, Gloria said, "You ready for the big shoot? I can't believe I'm going to be in my first movie."

"Crazy, huh?"

"Thank you so much, my love."

"Don't mention it," Johnny said as he floated over to her for another kiss. "Have you been practicing your lines?"

"I know that script like the back of my hand," she affirmed.

"Well, that's good. I need to reread it myself, to be honest," Johnny said.

"You better get on it, we can go over it together if you like," Gloria suggested.

"That sounds like a great idea, baby," he said as he swam across the pool to do a couple of laps. Because of his new bad habit, he swam nearly twice as fast as he did before. He swam four laps before he took a moment to breathe.

"You should take me out tonight," she said.

"Oh yeah? Where do you want to go?" Johnny asked.

"I don't know, maybe somewhere exotic for dinner. I want to eat some Columbian or some Peruvian food or something. I'm not sure what," Gloria said.

"Sure, wherever you want to go. There is this new Brazilian steakhouse that just opened up downtown. I've heard good things," Johnny said.

"Yum, that sounds perfect."

"All right, let me see if I can score us some reservations," Johnny said. He kissed her one more time before he swam away and got out of the pool.

149

Before he would go inside, he took a quick dip into the hot tub, which was sizzling. Trevor came out with a cold beer bottle and gave it to Johnny and said, "You better finish reading that script I gave you. I'm telling you, that one will win you a Best Actor of the Year award."

"All right, I will finish it as soon as possible, chief," Johnny said as he cracked open the beer and took a swig. Trevor climbed into the hot tub, too.

"Damn, that's hot as fuck, bruh," said Trevor jumping out of the water so only his feet were inside.

"I had the technician turn the temperature up a bit past regulation temp," Johnny said.

"Yeah, that's too fucking hot, we gotta turn that shit down," Trevor said before he got completely out of the tub and grabbed a towel.

"Suit yourself," Johnny said. After a couple of minutes, Johnny emerged from the tub and dried himself off. He wrapped a towel around his head.

Johnny went back inside the house and entered the living room. He took a seat by the couch, bent over, grabbed a rolled-up hundred-dollar bill and snorted a line of cocaine off of the center table. The powder shot up his nose so fast, Johnny could almost feel it go straight to his brain.

Then, Johnny felt his phone vibrating inside his pocket as his pulse sped up. He took it out and saw that it was Cole calling. Johnny picked up the phone after a few seconds of letting it ring.

"Hey Cole, what's going on?"

"What the fuck is up, superstar?" Cole asked.

"You know? Just hanging out with my fiancée and Trevor," Johnny responded.

"Bro, I finally got around to watching *Loose Ends*. And man, you really knocked it out of the park, my friend. I never knew you had it in you!"

"Thanks, Cole. I appreciate it," Johnny replied. He picked up a half of a joint from the ashtray on the coffee table and lit it. He inhaled the smoke slowly until the ember turned bright orange.

"Listen, I have this awesome new movie I'm doing next year that I think you would be perfect for. Want me to send you the script?" Cole asked.

"Yeah, perhaps. Why not? Send it over. Is it for stunts or…?"

"Nah, brother. This is a real role. It's a buddy cop flick, and we would costar together, actually," Cole said.

"Hmm, sounds cool. Is Don producing this one too?" Johnny asked.

"Man, fuck Don. That creepy fuck," said Cole.

"What now?" Johnny asked. "I thought that's your good buddy."

"Not anymore. Not after the crazy shit I been hearing about that asshole lately."

"Oh yeah? What's that?"

"Well, I don't even know if you'd believe me. But I'm done working with Don Steiner. Period. Some really weird shit is going on."

"What happened?" Johnny asked.

"It's kind of a long story. But I'll tell you this," Cole began to talk quieter. "A good friend of mine, Rosie Shoemaker, was set to do this movie with me, *Stars Among Us*. I got her an audition with Don a few months ago. A week goes by, I don't hear anything from her. Then, her family starts looking for her. Her sister called me, asking if I had seen her. She's been missing ever since, bro. And I think Don has something to do with it. I don't have any proof, but I just have a feeling. I've been hearing crazy conspiracies about him for a while now, something about him being involved in a sex trafficking ring or some shit. I don't know. Just wanted to tell you to be careful around that fucker."

"Wow, well I'm sorry to hear about your friend. But honestly, I highly doubt that Don Steiner of all people had anything to do with it," said Johnny. "That sounds just a bit batshit crazy, bro."

"It's all just a tad strange, you know?"

"It is, but honestly…he's been pretty good to me," Johnny said. "Not gonna bite the hand that feeds over some insane conspiracy theory."

"Just wanted to warn you, brother."

"Thanks, but I think I can take care of myself. Honestly, I think you're just trying to scare me out of doing my next movie with him because you're jealous," Johnny said with conviction before taking a big hit from the fat joint.

"Jealous?" Cole asked. "Chill the fuck out, Playboy. You're going to need a few more hit movies out before I get jealous of you!"

"A-huh. Sure. I bet you can't stand seeing me in the spotlight," Johnny said. "You know what, Cole? Fuck off. I got shit to do."

Johnny pressed the "end" button on the phone before throwing it onto the couch.

An angry look grew on Johnny's face. He picked up the television remote control and turned on the massive 85-inch flatscreen high-definition 4K masterpiece of technology mounted to the wall. A news channel was the first thing that appeared before Johnny changed it to Channel 4. He flipped through the channels until he landed on Channel 11. He noticed a commercial for something very familiar. It was the *Loose Ends* trailer. Johnny watched himself on his TV as it still amazed him to see himself so clearly. Not just a few seconds here and there like he would when he was just a stuntman. Johnny took a swig from his beer and watched as the commercial came to an end. "That's damn cool," he said to himself. Johnny sat on the couch and fell asleep about five minutes into one of his favorite cartoons growing up, *MoonMan*.

The following week, Johnny and Gloria began shooting their new movie, *Hang Nail,* written by one of the top horror writers in Hollywood, Keith Morino. Gloria played Johnny's girlfriend in the movie. Although she would end up dying halfway through, it was still a sizeable role for someone just getting into the film industry.

The first scene consisted of Johnny's character, Harrison, taking Gloria's character, Paula, to a drive-in theater. It was a big jump scare scene where the main killer in the movie, Hang Nail, tried to attack them before they were able to get away. Gloria was a big hit with everybody on set. Her personality was infectious; everybody loved her. The director, Scott Wiggins, even began to flirt with Gloria a little at one moment when they were talking. That is, until Johnny came by and shut it down completely, making Scott know his place with his fiancée.

Johnny and Gloria were relaxing and waiting for the next scene to shoot in their shared dressing room, something that Gloria asked Johnny to do so they could be together on set.

Gloria picked up a mirror. She took a rolled-up bill and snorted a line of premium Columbian cocaine. Johnny had gotten access to the most exclusive drug dealers in Hollywood, thanks to his agent, Cashew, who was quite the partaker himself.

"Damn," she said after she snorted her line.

"Take it easy," Johnny said. "We have to be able to still perform well."

Johnny's paranoia had increased greatly ever since he developed this affinity for the powdered stimulant. He was already quite paranoid at the thought of more people mistaking him for Cole and coming after him for money. Now, he had all sorts of paparazzi coming up and taking his picture and recording videos. Not to mention, all of the fans that would stop him and ask for pictures and autographs. The drugs helped him numb himself from all of the newfound anxiety he endured from this fresh burst of fame. But sometimes, it seemed to only make it worse.

Johnny unscrewed his prescription pill bottle and popped a couple of painkillers into his mouth. He chased them down with a bottle of sparkling water. He then joined Gloria in doing another line of coke.

A couple of minutes later, they heard a knock on the door. It was one of the production assistants. Johnny hid all of the drugs in cabinets before he opened the door.

"Hey there, you guys are needed for the next scene in ten minutes on Lot 10," the young man said.

"We'll be there," Johnny said.

"Thank you, sweetheart," Gloria said before slamming the door shut in his face.

Johnny and Gloria went on to film three more scenes that day. All of which were very well-received by the director, producers, crew, and everybody on set. Gloria was a natural. And Johnny was becoming quite the star among his peers. Everybody treated him with a new level of respect, especially with all of the success *Loose Ends* was seeing in the box office.

After filming had wrapped that night, Johnny and Gloria were escorted by security to the valet section in the back of the studio parking lot. Soon, the valet driver pulled up in Johnny's brand new Electroid 540Z. Its doors opened from the bottom and came up to the top and out like some sort of futuristic science-fiction movie. Johnny opened the passenger door for Gloria and held her hand as she got inside. Johnny walked around to the other side of the car, handed the valet a fifty-dollar bill, and got behind the wheel. He pushed a button on the dashboard and the doors slid back down and into place. Johnny pushed another button to put the car into drive, and then pushed a few more buttons, which made the car drive itself.

Johnny exited through the back gate and drove for a couple of miles before merging onto the highway. A few minutes later, Johnny noticed a suspicious black sedan following behind. It was getting closer and closer. Johnny took control of the wheel and turned off self-drive mode. He pushed the gas pedal down as hard as he could, accelerating the car from fifty to eighty miles per hour in 1.7 seconds. The black sedan followed behind closely.

"Shit," Johnny said to Gloria.

"What is it? What's going on?" she asked.

"I think we're being followed," Johnny replied. "Hold on."

Johnny swerved into the right lane and tried to gain a bit of distance from the car behind him. The sedan swerved into the same lane and sped up.

"Dammit, I've got to try something else," said Johnny as he swerved back into the left lane. He pushed the pedal down even further, accelerating the car to one-hundred miles per hour. He zoomed down the highway as the car followed from about forty feet behind. The car got close enough for Johnny to recognize the logo that was similar to the hexagonal logo on the van that tried to kidnap the little girl. *That's odd*, he thought to himself.

"I think I have an idea," Johnny said.

"I was waiting for you to say that!" Gloria exclaimed, gripping onto the handle on the roof of the car as Johnny whipped down the highway at one-hundred-five miles per hour. He weaved in and out of the lanes to avoid other cars on the highway. Finally, Johnny saw an exit about a mile away. He continued as fast as he could until he slowed the car down to eighty miles per hour to take control. The sedan followed closely, trying to ram into the back of Johnny's brand-new Electroid.

"Shit!" Johnny shouted. "Okay, hold on!"

Johnny downshifted into fourth gear before turning on turbo mode. He drove through two lanes to the right toward Exit 35. This made the black sedan stall for a second before trying to copy Johnny's maneuver. Just then, a large truck barreled into the black sedan, knocking it off the highway and onto the shoulder of the road. Johnny zoomed off the exit and continued to the stoplight before turning left. He managed to evade them entirely and found another route home on the car's GPS system. "That was too damn close," he said.

"Well, at least you saved us," Gloria said before reaching over and planting a kiss on Johnny's cheek. He continued down the backroads until they reached the driveway of their house.

Chapter Nineteen

The next morning, Johnny woke up before Gloria who was passed out on their king-sized bed snoring away. Johnny rose quietly, trying not to wake her. He walked outside of his bedroom and into the living room to find Trevor asleep on the couch with the video game controller still in his right hand. Johnny laughed to himself before he went to the refrigerator for a cold bottle of water. He unscrewed the cap and guzzled it down. He had a massive headache from partying the night before. Johnny walked down the hallway and into the bathroom.

Johnny blew his nose into the bathroom sink before he looked back up at himself in the mirror. He splashed his face with water a couple times before washing his hands with soap.

Johnny could not stop thinking about what Cole had told him about Don Steiner. Back in the living room, he opened his laptop and did some research trying to dig up any evidence that would corroborate Cole's story. But the only things he could find were various fringe theories posted on message boards and videos on StreamTube. Most of which had less than 200 views. Nothing definitive that would back up any of Cole's claims.

Johnny made some eggs, sausage and bacon in the kitchen. He was starving. The smell of the bacon woke up both Trevor and Gloria who eventually dragged themselves into the kitchen.

"Mmm, smells so good, babe," said Gloria before giving Johnny a kiss on the cheek.

"Hope you made enough for your boy," said Trevor.

"You already know," said Johnny as he scooped some scrambled eggs onto a plate for his best friend.

Trevor took a carton of pulp-free orange juice from the fridge and poured himself a full cup.

"Y'all want some?" Trevor asked as he began drinking the orange juice.

"Sure," said Gloria.

"I'm okay, I got coffee," said Johnny. "But I'm making you animals some plates right now. Hope you're hungry."

"Hell to the yeah," said Trevor.

The three of them ate breakfast together and laughed about the night before. Trevor had ended up getting so high and drunk, that he freestyle rapped for almost two hours for Johnny and Gloria. They loved it because Trevor was actually quite good at rapping.

After breakfast, Gloria and Johnny took a steaming hot shower together. They spent the morning binge-watching their favorite new show, *Monster High*. They were on season two, episode three. Gloria was lying in Johnny's arms on their bed, watching their humungous wall mounted 4K HD television.

Gloria looked up at Johnny and said, "Hey honey, I have to tell you something."

Johnny grabbed the remote control and pushed the pause button. "What's up, babe?"

"Well. I wish I had told you when it happened, but for some reason I was worried about how you would react," Gloria said. She sat up.

"What? What happened?" he asked.

"Nothing really. It's just. I feel guilty not saying anything. So, here it goes. When I auditioned for *Hang Nail* with Don Steiner a while back…well…how do I say this. He kind of tried to coerce me into sex. I mean. I don't know. It was really weird."

"What the fuck? Tell me you didn't," Johnny said as he stood up from the bed and backed away from her.

"No. I didn't touch him."

"Okay, phew."

"However," Gloria said as tears filled her eyes, "I did end up showing him my breasts for a couple of seconds. Please don't be mad. I guess it was enough for him to give me the part or whatever, I don't know. I'm so sorry, baby."

"God dammit. That son of a bitch!" Johnny shouted. He was quite shocked and angry to find this out. "So, you really didn't touch him or nothing? Just showed him your tits?"

Johnny looked at her with disgust.

"Yes, that's it. I swear. I would never touch that pig!"

Johnny paced back and forth down the hallway. Then, he stood in the corner and thought to himself for a few moments. Gloria began to cry more as tears dropped to her cheek. Johnny could see she was upset. He finally walked over and gave her a big hug.

"Ugh. Look. It's not your fault. He's a powerful piece of shit creep. You did what you felt you had to do. You wanted to be in our movie that bad. I just wish he did not put you through that. I can't believe that Cole was right about him all along. I should have listened. Fuck. And now we're making this movie for him. God dammit! I want to beat his ass so bad right now."

"Baby don't do anything that is going to get you into any trouble. I'm so sorry, I know I should have told you sooner," Gloria said.

"Yeah maybe. But I understand why you wouldn't. I just can't believe it. I wonder if Cole is actually right about this other girl, Rosie."

"Who is Rosie?" she asked.

"Well, I don't really know. I guess she went missing after Cole set her up for an audition with Don. Cole thinks that Don has something to do with it. Something to do with sex trafficking, I don't really know. I honestly wasn't really paying attention or listening that well because I thought Cole was just fucking with me. But holy fuck, what if Don is really involved in that shit?"

"That's crazy! What if that happened to me? I got such an eerie vibe around that guy; I would not doubt it now that I think about it."

"Maybe we should do something," said Johnny.

"Like what could we do? And wouldn't that ruin everything with *Hang Nail*? With him being the lead executive producer and all?" Gloria asked. Johnny used his shirt to help wipe her eyes.

"I don't know, but I don't feel like I can stand back and do nothing," Johnny said. He was holding back his rage.

Johnny walked over to their dresser. Laid on top was a mirror containing a few long lines of cocaine and a rolled-up hundred-dollar bill. Johnny used it to snort one of the lines of powder.

"I just want to beat that motherfucking ugly simp's ass," Johnny fumed, pacing back and forth.

"I understand, sweetie," said Gloria. She joined him and did a line of cocaine herself. Johnny gave Gloria a kiss and said, "I love you, baby. Give me a second, I need to talk to Cole really quick."

Johnny walked into the living room and sat down on the couch. He pulled out his phone and texted Cole, "Hey man, sorry I low key spazzed on you yesterday."

A couple of minutes passed before he got a text back. It was from Cole. It read, "Don't sweat it, bozo. No worries at all. I get it."

"I can't believe it, but I think you were right."

"About what? I'm right all the time?" Cole texted back.

"Well, at least about Don being a complete creep fuck," Johnny texted.

"How'd you find out?" Cole replied.

"I just learned he made a move on my fiancée, Gloria, a while back. I'm not sure about all the other stuff you were talking about. But I believe you, he's a piece of shit. I want to fuck him up," Johnny texted back.

"Damn, man. That's crazy. Sorry to hear. Well, hate to say I told you so. But yeah, fuck him. He's a filthy rich loser of a human being, and he deserves to have his nuts chopped tf off," Cole wrote.

"If I see Don on set tomorrow, I may not be able to stop myself from cracking his jaw," Johnny wrote.

"Bahaha," Cole typed back. "I don't blame you. Hey, listen, I just wanted to let you know that I paid off all the bookies I owed. So, you should not have those dickhead goons on your back anymore. I was trying to tell you yesterday before you hung up on me. But again, I get it."

"Word, it's no problem. I didn't even really mind, it was fun beating the shit out of them, to be honest," Johnny texted.

"Hahaa, you wild son of a gun," Cole wrote.

"Well, I gotta run," Johnny wrote. "Let's hang out soon, maybe get a bite to eat or some shit."

"Sounds like a plan," Cole wrote back. "Also, I'm sending you that script. I really want you in this movie with me."

"Send it over, bro."

"Will do."

Johnny put his phone in his pocket. He stood up from the couch and returned to Gloria in their bedroom and gave her a hug around her waste from behind. They laid back down on the bed. Johnny picked up the remote control and pressed play. They continued to watch some more *Monster High*.

The next day, Johnny and Gloria got a ride to set from Trevor who quit his day job to fully commit to supporting Johnny and helping him in any way he could. When they got to the studio parking lot, Johnny was tense sitting in the front seat of the Electroid.

"You good, bro?" Trevor asked Johnny as he pulled the car into an empty parking spot.

Once they were all signed in up front, Gloria and Johnny were escorted to their dressing room.

Trevor accompanied them, because Johnny had filled him in on what happened with Don, and he wanted Trevor to have his back on set that day. Johnny just told people he was his new private security guard.

Inside their joint dressing room, Johnny, Gloria, and Trevor snorted lines of cocaine and took shots of distilled vodka. Trevor was sitting in the corner rolling up a big blunt for Johnny and him to enjoy. Gloria was called to the makeup station. Johnny and Trevor stayed back. Once Trevor was done rolling up the thick cigar full of strong ganja, the two of them went out back behind the trailer.

"This shit is called Hawaiian Hopscotch," Trevor said as he lifted a lighter from his pocket and sparked it up. He torched the end of the blunt until it was completely lit. Trevor inhaled the smoke. He took a few more hits before he passed it over to Johnny. Johnny's nerves were running wild; he needed something to help balance out his anxiety and the cocaine. The combination of substances was definitely taking an effect.

As soon as they finished the blunt, Johnny had to go to the bathroom. He returned to the studio and entered through a back door. On his way down the long hall, he noticed Don Steiner with a beautiful female who Johnny assumed was another aspiring actress of some sort.

"Hey Don!" Johnny called.

"Johnny! My main star!" Don said as he walked closer. The girl he was with looked petrified to be in the producer's presence. The simple sight of the rather large movie mogul disgusted Johnny to no end. But he tried to hide it for the time being.

"Listen, we need to talk," Johnny said.

"Sure, walk with us," said Don as he continued down the hallway with the frightened young actress wrapped around his arm.

"Don, I'm serious, hold up," said Johnny as he followed him. Don pushed through the door that led to the production area where most of the cast and crew were hanging out getting ready to film for the day.

"What is it, Mister Biggs?" Don asked as he turned around and looked at Johnny.

Johnny cleared his throat. "Gloria just told me how she got the role for the movie. She told me you tried to get her to have sex with you. And when she wouldn't, you made her show her boobs or some shit!" Johnny shouted. "What in the hell is wrong with you? Is that true?"

"Whoa, those are some bold accusations!" Don responded. The actress next to him distanced herself a few feet from Don Steiner who had visually became unsettled. "Who the fuck are you to come at me with this shit?"

"I'm her god damn fiancée. So, is it true or not?"

"Look, I honestly don't even remember our meeting all that well. You know with old age; we get forgetful sometimes. But I do remember something, yeah, that's right, she did show me her goods," Don said with an evil grin on his face. "Nice rack she has too, by the way. Kudos to you, pal."

The crowd of actors, actresses, and crew gathered around and watched as Johnny confronted the producer.

"And what happened to Rosie Shoemaker, huh?" Johnny asked.

Gasps were heard among the crowd. Don began to clearly turn red.

"I have no clue what you're going on about, boy, but you better watch your tone, or I'll have you ended in this town. Finished!"

"What did you do to Rosie Shoemaker?" Johnny asked again.

"You better shut your damn mouth," Don Steiner said. "Whatever did happen to little Rosie, we don't want the same thing happening to your slut of a girlfriend now, do we?"

Johnny cocked his fist back in a ball and punched Don Steiner across the jaw, knocking him to the ground. Don got back up to his feet, grabbed a chair and threw it at Johnny. Johnny ducked, and punched him again, this time in the right eye. Don fell back, and the crew hurried forward to break the two apart. They pulled Johnny away just as Gloria was walking back, too busy from getting her makeup done to notice what was going on.

As they were pulling him off of Don, Johnny shouted, "You fucking creep! What happened to Rosie Shoemaker?"

"You're done! You're fired, motherfucker! See if you ever get a job in Hollywood again!" Don yelled as his eye began to swell up and turn black and blue.

Security finally ran in and grabbed Johnny before wrestling him to the ground.

"Get that asshole out of here, I want him arrested!" Don said. Security dragged Johnny away, with Gloria following behind. Trevor, meanwhile, had returned to the studio and heard the commotion. Once he got closer, he punched Don in the face. Don dropped back down to the ground. Trevor ran away quickly before security could apprehend him, too. He followed Gloria, who followed behind the security guard escorting Johnny out of the studio. When they

165

reached the back parking lot, the security guard let Johnny go.

"What? You're not gonna call the police?" Johnny asked.

"Nah, just get out of here. I hate that douchebag, Don Steiner. I've heard some weird shit about that dude. Always seeing him with women leaving his office like he just did something truly terrible to them. Fuck that guy," the security guard said. Trevor took out the keys to the Electroid as the three of them walked to the car. Gloria got in the back, while Johnny and Trevor got in the passenger and the driver seat. Trevor pushed the start button and the electric engine hummed. Trevor exited the parking lot and headed home.

Johnny pulled out his phone and gave it to Gloria. "Record this."

"Huh? Okay. Whatever you say, sweetie," she said as she pulled up the camera app on the phone and pressed the record button.

"Hey world. My name is Johnny Biggs, Actor and Stuntman. And I have a message and public service announcement about my former boss, Don Steiner. This guy is a fucking sexual harassment nightmare. He harassed my fiancée. I'm sure he's done it to hundreds if not thousands of women over the decades that this asshole has been in the industry. I have also gotten word that he may be involved in a sex trafficking ring of some sort. I don't have any evidence, but I'm pretty sure it's true. I am asking you, everybody watching, for the women that he has hurt to come out and tell their story. Because a lot of women may be getting hurt because of this man. Where the hell is Rosie Shoemaker? I hope all of his victims come out and this man is stopped! He may have given me a job as an actor, but he is a terrible human being that needs to be stopped now! I am asking all of you for your help. Let's put an end to this motherfucker!"

Johnny finished talking and Gloria pressed the "end" button on the phone to stop recording.

"I'm going to upload that to all of my social media accounts. Hopefully that helps in some way," Johnny said.

"Damn," Gloria said. She seemed panicked at the situation, but she felt safe with Johnny. "I love you so much, baby. My acting career may be over before it even started, but I am proud of you," Gloria said before giving Johnny his phone back. Then, she leaned over to the front seat to give him a big kiss on the lips.

"Don't worry, darling. I will make sure you still have a career," Johnny said. "I promise."

Chapter Twenty

A few days later, Johnny and Gloria were out to the movies at the local theater. They were seeing *Trailblazers Anonymous*, a romantic comedy starring Johnny's good friend, Cole Tillman.

When the movie ended, they headed down the long hall of theaters. Gloria looked at the posters on the wall, dreaming that would be her one day. Unfortunately, the production of *Hang Nail* was put on hold while the studio figured out what to do after all of the controversy surrounding Don and Johnny.

"That *Trailblazers* movie was actually quite good," Gloria said. "I mean, I liked it at least."

"You know what, I agree. That was quite awesome. I should call Cole later and tell him," Johnny replied.

"Any word on what's going on with *Hang Nail?*" Gloria asked with anticipation in her tone.

"Not yet, honey. You know I'll let you know as soon as I hear. But I have a feeling everything is going to work out. Somehow. Just trust me."

"Okay, I trust you," said Gloria as she held Johnny's hand. They continued past the concession stands and ticket takers. The movie theater was packed full.

"Johnny Biggs!" one person yelled.

"Ah shit," Johnny said as they walked outside.

"Is that really Johnny Biggs?" Nearby fans swarmed around Johnny and Gloria.

"Can I get a selfie?" a middle schooler asked.

"Uhh, yeah, I guess," said Johnny as he turned and posed for a pic with the fan.

Another woman walked up and pretty much forced herself on Johnny before snapping a picture with her phone. A mother and daughter asked for an autograph, putting a marker in front of Johnny's face. He signed their ticket stub as they were going to watch *Loose Ends*. Gloria stood to the side with a tad bit of jealousy as the crowd bombarded Johnny, giving him all this attention. Johnny continued to interact with the fans and take photos and sign things for several minutes.

Gloria was getting a bit restless waiting for Johnny to finish up with his fans when her phone pinged with a text message from her friend Lisa, prompting Gloria to walk away from the crowd for a moment. She was about ten feet away from Johnny when she started texting Lisa back.

A hooded man ran out of the shadows and grabbed Gloria. She screamed, but the voices of the crowd muffled her voice, so Johnny did not hear at first.

He took one more selfie with a fan. Then, in the camera of the phone staring back at him, he could see somebody dragging Gloria toward a van on the street. Johnny immediately took off after them.

The hooded man threw Gloria into the back of the van before hopping inside and slamming the door shut. The van took off.

"No!" Johnny yelled.

169

A sedan pulled up to park in front of the movie theater where the van had just been parked.

Johnny jumped inside the car. "Please, for the love of God, let me borrow this car. That van just took my fiancée!"

"Oh my gosh, you're Johnny Biggs! Of course, here you go," said the middle-aged man. He quickly got out, and Johnny slid behind the wheel. He put the pedal to the medal and followed the shady black van down the road.

As Johnny adjusted his seat and mirrors, he made sure to keep the van in sight. He got up to about twenty feet behind the van before it made a sharp right turn onto Monroe Boulevard. Johnny followed behind and made a sharp right turn as well. Just then, lightning struck, and it began to pour down rain.

The sedan hydroplaned. But that did not stop Johnny. He tailed the van for about two miles before it merged onto the highway. Johnny drove the sedan up the highway ramp and stepped on the accelerator, taking the car to eighty-five miles per hour. "That van's not stopping for nothing," Johnny muttered.

Johnny got the car about fifteen away from the van before its side door opened and a man in a black ski mask and hoodie positioned himself out of the van, holding onto the side. He pulled up a pistol and started shooting. Bullets ricocheted off of the sedan and into traffic. One bullet struck the left side-view mirror. Johnny ducked to avoid any shots to his face or body. The man finally climbed back inside the van and slammed the side door. Johnny lifted back up to see bullet holes in the windshield. He continued to follow close behind.

Inside the van, Gloria's eyes were blindfolded, and her mouth taped shut. Her hands were tied behind her back with a rope. One man stayed with her to make sure that she did not try to get away.

"I don't think your boyfriend is going to get to us, sweetie," the masked man said. "Don't worry, we'll take good care of you."

Gloria tried to speak, but her mouth was covered with tape, so the man could not make out what she was saying.

"The place you are going is really, really, nice," the man said as the van sped up. "You're going to love it there. A lot of girls just like you, you will all get along well."

The shadowy man laughed. He pushed Gloria to the side and grabbed a heavy machine gun. "Hope your boyfriend can handle this one."

The man opened the side door, held onto the handlebar, and released a torrent of bullets at the sedan behind them.

"Oh shit!" Johnny said, swerving into the left lane. He had to slow down before ducking behind the wheel. Shots flew everywhere around him. A couple hit the side of the car. After about ten seconds, the bullets stopped coming and the van picked up speed. Johnny pushed the pedal down hard and pulled up closer to the van.

A state trooper's radar gun read ninety-three miles per hour when the van passed him, followed by Johnny who was near the same speed. The trooper jumped into his cruiser and began to chase after Johnny.

Johnny continued down the highway, the rain coming down ever harder. He was about ten feet from the van when lightning struck as loud as a gunshot nearby.

Inside the van, Gloria tried to fight back. She charged at the man, but her arms and legs were tied with rope, and she fell down on her face. Just then, the masked man struck her across the cheek with the butt of his assault rifle.

"Are you serious, bitch?" the guy said. He kicked her with his booted foot . "Move again and you're dead."

Johnny looked in his rear-view mirror and saw the state trooper had turned on his red and blue lights and was gaining on him. Johnny continued to chase the van. "Not stopping for nothing and no one," he said out loud. Finally, the van came to a congested part of the highway with a little bit of traffic. The van swerved around a truck and onto the right shoulder of the highway. Johnny did the same maneuver and almost drove straight into the guard rail before he regained control of the sedan.

The state trooper followed the car chase, trying to catch up to both cars which were not stopping. The trooper had called for backup. Soon, two more state troopers joined the chase.

The van driver saw that a government truck was blocking the shoulder as they were doing road work up ahead. Yellow lights flashed as the traffic got even slower. The van slowed down as it had nowhere to go. Johnny was not slowing down...he drove the sedan into the back of the van at nearly fifty miles an hour.

The sedan tore through the back of the van and the airbag exploded into Johnny's face. He was barely buckled up at that point, so the airbag saved his life. After a few moments of confusion, Johnny undid the seat belt and kicked open the driver's side door. Johnny stumbled out of the car and ran toward the van before its side door flung open and pistol bullets flew. Johnny hid behind one of the highway work trucks.

The man shot four more times before he realized Johnny was nowhere to be found.

The man looked to the right, and saw Johnny leap up onto another one of the cars. Johnny dove off, kicking the hooded man in the throat and dropping him to the ground. Johnny took the pistol and threw it off the road before it bounced into dirt. He got on top of the man and punched him twice, knocking him out cold. Johnny pulled the latch of the side door and ripped it open. He saw Gloria lying there tied up and mouth taped.

"Gloria!" He picked her up and pulled her out. The van had that same logo on it that Johnny had been seeing all over and even on some of Don's paperwork. The state troopers ran up with their guns drawn. "Freeze! Nobody move!" one of the troopers shouted as he pointed his gun at Johnny and Gloria. They both dropped to the ground.

"Don't shoot!" Johnny pleaded. "I was just saving her from those assholes!" Johnny pointed toward the man on the ground. Another man in a ski mask emerged from the van with his hands up but had a change of heart and tried to run away. One of the state troopers shot the man in the leg, making him fall flat to the ground. Another officer went over to assist Gloria who was still tied up with tape over her mouth.

"We're gonna need a medic! Call for an ambulance!" the officer yelled. The other state troopers arrested the masked men. Johnny carefully removed the tape from Gloria's mouth.

"Hey baby," she said once her mouth was free.

"Hey beautiful," he said with cuts all over his face from the crash. Johnny planted a big kiss on her lips as the rain fell down upon them.

"You're my hero, you saved me," Gloria said. Johnny took out his pocketknife and cut the ropes, freeing her hands and feet.

"I'd do anything for you," Johnny replied as he held her close.

"We're gonna take you guys down to the local hospital, we'll get your statement there," said one of the officers.

"That's fine," said Johnny.

"Thank you," Gloria said.

"Don't mention it, darling." He held her close until the ambulance showed up to take them to the hospital.

Johnny and Gloria stayed at the hospital for a few hours as doctors and nurses checked their vitals and did different types of tests. They were mostly fine, aside from a few bad cuts that Johnny had to get stitched up from the crash. Gloria had some scratches and a big black eye but overall, she was okay.

"You're two tough individuals," the doctor told Gloria and Johnny as they laid in their dual hospital beds.

"No shit, that's Johnny Biggs, and future Mrs. Biggs!" Gloria said as she held her ribs in pain.

Trevor picked up his friends when they were ready to be discharged. Gloria and Johnny got inside the Pompa back seat together. Johnny put his arm around Gloria as Trevor drove them all back home.

A week later, Johnny and Trevor were sitting on the couch playing *League of Shooters* on the big screen HD television when Johnny got a phone call.

"What's going on, Cole?"

"Bro, how the hell are you?"

"I guess I'm all right, how about you?"

"Hey, by the way, I read the script for *Lit City,* and it is fucking awesome. Hell yeah, I'll do it with you," Johnny said.

"That's great to hear, John. But listen. Turn on your TV right now. Turn on the news channel," said Cole.

Johnny turned on the news to see a video of a large mansion being raided by police. The title on the bottom read, "Hollywood Sex Trafficking Ring Shut Down."

"Whoa," said Johnny.

He turned up the volume to hear what the reporter was saying. "Police have uncovered the location of a local sex trafficking compound in the basement of none other than famed Hollywood producer, Don Steiner's estate hidden in the woods. It was one of many of the film mogul's homes, but this one had over a dozen women kidnapped and held against their will in the basement of the mansion."

"Holy shit," Trevor said before dropping his jaw.

The reporter went on to say, "Thanks to a viral video posted by actor and stuntman, Johnny Biggs, calling on all of Steiner's victims to come forward, police were able to gather enough evidence and intel to locate the whereabouts of the missing girls. One girl, Rosie Shoemaker, had been missing for months. Rosie's family was pleased to find that Rosie was still alive, but barely as she was held against her will and sold off to rich men for sex for months on end.

"Thankfully, this nightmare is now over for Rosie and many girls like her. Girls who just wanted to become movie stars and were victimized at the hands of Don Steiner and his associates. Let's go now live to Jim Matthews, who is reporting from the precinct where Don Steiner is believed to have been arrested just a few moments ago."

A shot switched to Don Steiner being handcuffed and escorted to the back of a police car.

"You did it, motherfucker," Cole said.

"Damn, that's wild," Johnny replied. "I can't believe it. That could have been Gloria."

"Thank you for being such a badass, thank you for having Rosie found. I hope she can forgive me," said Cole.

"It's not your fault, you were only trying to help her live her dreams," said Johnny. "Maybe put her in one of your next movies or something."

"Not a bad idea. Maybe we can find a role for Gloria in *Lit City* as well."

"That would be awesome. I gotta run, talk soon, okay?"

"Sounds good, brother. Take care of yourself," said Cole.

"Likewise," Johnny replied.

A couple of days later, Johnny and Gloria received a group chat call from the other producers of *Hang Nail*. One of them, Kurt Little, told Johnny that they still planned to move forward with the film without Don Steiner on board, considering the fact that he was now in county jail. They all apologized profusely for what happened to Gloria, and even offered to double both their salaries if they would stay on board. Johnny said to leave his alone but to give Gloria triple what they'd originally promised. They obliged, and the two went back to finish filming the horror flick.

Johnny made sure to find the fan that had loaned him the car to chase down Gloria's kidnappers. He knew the car was totaled, so he gifted the fan with his Electroid self-driving vehicle. The fan was overjoyed and grateful. Johnny also took some pictures with him and his family and signed multiple autographs for them.

One afternoon, Johnny, Gloria, and Trevor were driving down the road. Trevor was in the driver's seat, Johnny in the back, and Gloria was in the passenger seat of the Pompa SUV. Trevor was going over a bridge when Johnny said, "Hey pull over for a second."

Trevor pulled over and Johnny got out. He walked to the edge of the bridge that overlooked a small river. Trevor and Gloria both got out of the car to see what Johnny was doing.

"I don't need this shit anymore," Johnny said as he reached into his pockets. He pulled out a decent sized bag of cocaine. He held it in the air and said, "Fuck this," before dumping the bag into the water below. The powdered drug fell like snow during a winter blizzard. He then reached into his other pocket and took out his bottle of pain pills. "Goodbye, old friend," he said as he threw the bottle as far as he could into the water. Gloria hugged him tight from behind.

Trevor then said, "Fuck it, I guess I should too," before he reached into his pocket to take out a big blunt that he had rolled before they left the house. But just before he could toss it, Johnny stopped him and said, "Hold up, hold up."

"What's up?" Trevor asked.

"Weed isn't that bad. I say we save that for later," Johnny said.

"I guess you're right," Trevor said. Johnny and Gloria held hands as they walked back to the car. Trevor drove the SUV across the bridge and onto the road.

"So, what do you guys want to do today?" Trevor asked as he turned left onto Madison Court.

"Honestly, I don't even care. I just want a day to relax if you ask me," Johnny said.

"How about we go see a movie or something?" Gloria asked before laughing.

"I think I'm done with movies for a while, if that's okay. Let's go watch some football or basketball or some shit," said Johnny.

"Shit, Pro Wrestling is cool again. We can watch some of that?" Trever said with a smile.

"Not a bad idea, just anything besides film for a bit."

"I agree, that's a good idea," said Trevor.

"All right, fine, but Friday you're taking me to a movie," Gloria said to Johnny.

"We'll see, baby. We'll see," said Johnny.

Just then, Johnny felt his phone vibrating in his pocket. He took it out and saw that it was his agent, Cashew Peters.

"Cashew, what's going on?"

"Johnny! Listen! I hope all is well!"

"Not too bad," Johnny said as he looked at his fiancée and his best friend. "How are you?"

"Great! Thanks for asking. Listen, I just got a call about a project that the studio is working on. Apparently, there is a script in the works for a movie about you," Cashew said.

"Huh?" Johnny said. "What do you mean?"

"Yeah, apparently screenwriter and director, Teddy Lawson, wants to make a film about your life."

"Whoa," Johnny said. "That's weird. Why me?"

"Well, I don't know ya big dummy. Maybe because your story is insane. Because you went from being in the background to the spotlight. Maybe because you saved that girl and went viral? I don't know. But you are a badass and he wants to make a movie about you. So, I just need to know if you are okay with it, and I'll send you the paperwork about your likeness and story and all that."

"Hmm. Yeah, I guess that's fine, sounds pretty cool actually. Why not? Sure. Send over whatever you need to," Johnny said.

"Okay. But here's the wild part. Guess who they want to play you in the movie. You're never gonna guess," Cashew said with excitement in his voice.

"I have no clue. Tell me. Who?" Johnny asked.

"Cole Tillman."

Johnny paused for a second and then began to laugh. He stopped laughing and put the phone back up to his ear.

"No way. That's crazy, for real?" Johnny said as a smirk grew on his face.

"For real, and apparently, he has already agreed to it," Cashew said.

"Wow. That's pretty cool," Johnny said.

"Yeah, pretty fucking cool if you ask me," his agent said. "We'll iron out all the deets soon. But I gotta go, I'll talk to you soon, John."

"Talk to you later."

Johnny pressed the "End" button on the phone before putting it back into his pocket.

"Everything good?" Trevor asked.

"Yeah, bro. Everything is good. Turn the music up and let's go get something to eat."

"Hell yeah, I'm starving," Trevor said. He pushed down on the gas pedal and turned up the volume on the radio.

About the Author

JEFF YAGER grew up in Stamford, Connecticut, before relocating more than a decade ago to Florida, where he lives with his partner Justyna and their three sons in a town outside of Tampa. He has an associate degree from Pasco-Hernandez State College. In addition to his writing career, Jeff is a professional wrestler as well as a rap singer with several albums of his original songs available through CD Baby.

Jeff's published works include five novels besides *Stunt Double*: *Seven Days in Virtual Reality; Botanica,* co-authored with Fred Yager; *I Like God,* co-authored with Skye Bynes, a novel about social media; the YA novel *Atom & Eve;* and *A Ghostly Twist,* a YA novel (forthcoming). He also has published two children's books: *The Question is Why?* inspired by his son Bradley when he was a toddler; and *Chuck and Alfonzo,* about the unlikely friendship between a monkey and a dog. Both children's books are illustrated by Nancy Batra.

For more on Jeff, go to: https://jeffyager.us

Other books by Jeff Yager

Novels

Seven Days in Virtual Reality
Available in e-book, print, and audiobook versions.
Louis Parker is the divorced father of two teenagers who is still trying to find his life's purpose. After losing his job, Louie's financial situation convinces him he has nothing to lose if he agrees to test out a radical new virtual reality videogame for a substantial fee. But Louie quickly learns that virtual reality is a lot more complicated than he realized when Version 2 proves to be dramatically different from Version 1. When the testing ends, is Louie trapped in virtual reality forever? If he is able to return to his own reality, is it the same one he started from, or has it changed immeasurably?

Praise for *SEVEN DAYS IN VIRTUAL REALITY:*
"Jeff Yager's novel, *Seven Days in Virtual Reality*, is timely and provocative. Yager's characters and plot are sure to stay with you as you get to explore the wonders and intrigue of virtual reality."—Jeffrey J. Fox, bestselling author

Botanica

Available in e-book and print formats

What if we could communicate with the secret world of plants? What do you think they'd tell us about the planet they share with us? In this environmental thriller, biogenetics engineer Jason Woods finds that he's able to do just that after he's blasted with plant DNA in an accident involving a Gene Gun explosion in an R&D lab where genetically modified plants are created.

One of the after-effects is that he's able to plug into the vast network through which plants communicate. He enhances this communication through psychedelic mushrooms he buys at a Botanica.

The trees warn Jason that the earth is on the brink of another mass extinction event, like what happened to dinosaurs, and that the world of plants is using lethal methods to stop it.

Joining Jason on this amazing journey are Carter Wiseman, a befuddled FBI Agent investigating a series of plant-related deaths, Dr. Julie Green, a botany professor Wiseman recruits to help him, Sal, a son Jason never even knew he had, and a hitch-hiking environmental activist named Gypsy, not to mention a world of plants led by General Sherman, the oldest and tallest redwood in California's Sequoia National Park.

Welcome to *BOTANICA*, where you will never look at plants the same way again.

Praise for *BOTANICA*:

"I just finished *BOTANICA*. Loved the book. Kudos to the authors. Such talent! Such wisdom!! Inspiring as well."
—Sue M., teacher, book club member/organizer

I Like God

Available in e-book, print, and audiobook versions.

Joey Taylor jokingly starts a public page for "God" on FaceSpace and forgets about it when he goes off the grid from social media. Four years later, he returns to the page to find that it has over 30 million "likes." When Joey discovers the immense power and responsibility that comes with this incredible online audience at his disposal, the former pizza delivery driver develops a God complex of his own. Joey's newfound fame on FaceSpace takes a turn nobody could ever see coming.

Reviews:

"I Like God: A Novel" is one of those impressively written works of fiction that reveals something of what could really come to pass in today's social media dominated popular culture. A ripping great read from beginning to end, "I Like God: A Novel" is very highly recommended for community library General Fiction collections. For personal reading lists it should be noted that "I Like God: A Novel" is also available in a paperback edition (9781938998157, $14.95) and in a Kindle format ($5.99).—Micah Andrew, Reviewer (Midwest Book Review)

Atom & Eve

Available in e-book, print, and audiobook versions.

They say truth is stranger than fiction and ATOM & EVE, the prophetic novel about a deadly pandemic with no cure, is an example of that. In Yager's first sci-fi thriller, set several years in the future, sixteen-year-old Ricky Romanello, a college freshman, is playing basketball when he collapses and winds up in a coma suffering from a powerful flu that hits the U.S. population causing deaths and a dramatic economic slowdown. Research scientist Dr. Mandy Fox has been developing an anti-aging drug that she believes might also eradicate the flu. Ricky takes the drug and so does the rest of the population—until everyone soon discovers the unintended side effect to the new drug.

In this page-turner of a sci-fi novel, you'll also discover the first female presidential candidate and a police officer with questionable ethics. The way the author weaves together the plots and subplots of this intriguing debut novel is a memorable read that is appealing to adults as well as teens. *ATOM & EVE* has been translated and published in Japanese.

Praise for *ATOM & EVE*:

"A great debut for its author, Jeff Yager. Its mix of suspense, science, romance, and even politics will keep the reader turning the pages to find out what happens next, and there are enough twists and turns to ensure the pace never slackens."
—Alan Caruba, Editor, Bookviews.com, Founding member of the National Book Critics Circle

My Lucky Hat
A Short Story
Jeff Yager
Available as an e-book with an audiobook version narrated and produced by Russell D. Bernstein

Have you ever had a piece of clothing, or an object, that you thought brought you luck? Keenan, a college student, rediscovers the red hat that his Dad originally bought for him at a flea market when he was twelve. But can a hat really be lucky?

Children's Books

The Question is Why?
Written by Jeff Yager
Illustrated by Nancy Batra
Ages 2-6

Available in e-book, hardcover and paperback print editions

By a certain age, most children become very curious and they start asking "Why?" When a parent, teacher, or grandparent responds with an answer, these inquisitive children will often respond with another "Why?" *The Question is Why?* was inspired by the author's son, Bradley. In this fun and unique illustrated children's book, there are 26 different questions and answers, each corresponding to a letter of the alphabet. The book includes an illustrated alphabet chart, suggested books for further reading, and a list of fun activities.

Praise for *THE QUESTION IS WHY?*

"*The Question is Why?* incorporates both creative questioning AND an innovative take on learning the alphabet. It will make a great addition to any Pre-K or K-3 classroom library!"
—Kaitlin Roig-DeBellis, author, *Choosing Hope*; former first grade teacher, Sandy Hook Elementary School; and Executive Director, Classes4classes.org

La Pregunta Es Por Que?
Jeff Yager
Ilustrado para Nancy Batra
Spanish version of *The Question is Why?*
Translated by Karen Raicher and Adriana de Almeida
Navarro
2020

A los ninos les gusta preguntar "por que?" Esta
encantador libro ilustrado para ninos tiene las respuestas,
de la A a la Z.